Please feel free to
publisher filters th

Jamiee Lynne - jamiee_lynne@awesomeauthors.org

Sign up for my blog for updates and freebies!
jamiee.lynne.awesomeauthors.org

About the Publisher

BLVNP Incorporated, A Nevada Corporation, 340 S. Lemon #6200, Walnut CA 91789, info@blvnp.com / legal@blvnp.com

DISCLAIMER

King of Beasts

By: Jamiee Lynne

BLVNP

ISBN: 978-1-68030-817-4

Table of Contents

Dedication

For Haley, for inspiring me to always be better and for trying to convince me I was already the best

FREE DOWNLOAD

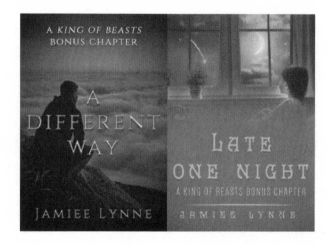

Get these freebies and MORE when you sign up for the author's mailing list!

jamiee.lynne.awesomeauthors.org

Chapter 1

If you can see them, then you're already dead. If you can hear them, then you're not far from it. If you can smell them, like the forest they live in, then avoid danger at all conceivable costs.

Because they're the monsters in the shadows of Harvey Hill's forests, and their king needs his queen.

In the deepest hours of the night, when the moon was as powerful as it could be, the beasts lurked. Crawling through the streets of the tiny, secluded town, they passed the doors marked with their symbols and took the offerings at the edge of the town's limits. On all fours, as they usually traveled beneath the moon, they were lithe and lethal, and the residents of

Harvey's Hill listened to their claws scraping over the tarmac while they pretended to be asleep.

No one wanted to be the next Ann Marie, or the next Jessica, or the girl from last week, Clair. They wanted their windows closed and a red symbol painted on their door to ward against the evil. They wanted ammonia on their doorsteps to hide their scents lest a beast finds them… appetizing and worth the effort of getting past the ward. And most certainly, they didn't want to be the mothers, fathers, sisters, or brothers who wake in the morning to find one bed empty within their house and footprints that seem like men's feet, caked in dirt, leading to their loved one's bedroom.

Here in Harvey's Hill, when the clock hits ten, you best be inside, under covers, and praying to the moon that the beasts will pretend you're not there.

That was what Charlotte has been doing for the past twenty years. She took her online courses so she won't risk a class running late at the community college three towns over. She didn't party because the other girls were usually taken from a risky gathering, passed out drunk by a bonfire. Charlotte painted the symbol on her family's door herself because she loved to draw… even if it means warding off the thing of her little town's nightmares, and she went through the exhausting training by the elders to learn the protective symbols, all of them, vested to only those capable of handling their magic. It has taken her years to learn them from her grandmother.

She got the best grades, was the best daughter, and had the best little brother in the entire world. Her dog, Gilmore, was an asshole, but she loved the ridiculous husky, and she swam in the local creek for hours.

But Charlotte lived in a small town with more woods than houses and more wild animals than not. And because they didn't know any better, a deer decided to cross the road just as Charlotte was coming back into town lines.

The sun had already descended, and the beasts were surly waiting for the clock to strike ten to make their appearance. She has been driving fast. It was eight. Sure, she still had two hours, but she needed to pour ammonia on their driveway and front steps still, draw the symbol on her door, and close the shades. In her mind, it didn't register that her family, realizing she was late, had already done all those things. She was speeding because it was all she knew to do.

She has been damning the stupid conference she was attending even though the discussion on hybridized energy development was fascinating to her. She was damning the speaker for giving her five minutes afterward even though she practically begged to speak to the professor. She was damning the fact that he found her smart enough, interesting enough, to talk for the next hour and a half while the sun made its effortless journey downwards.

And when the deer came from nowhere as they usually did, she damned her brakes, and her tires, and the road, and the fact it was past sundown and no cars would be passing by until sunrise. No one would see her and her car, no one would find her.

It was past dark, after all, and it was the beast's time to roam.

Chapter 2

The king let his wolves roam while he stood at the town line, naked and crouched low to the earth in human form. His fingers absentmindedly grabbed the dirt and leaves beneath his feet as he inhaled deeply and exhaled slowly.

The night smelled divine as though something else rode in the winds. He felt hungry. There was a howl in the distance, a victorious sound, and the king smiled. There was another mate found, another pack member to join.

He knew the settlers of this tiny town didn't understand what they agreed to by signing the pact. They overestimated their magic and underestimated the beasts. They crossed his lands, destroyed his forest, and stole his game. Two hundred years later, he was still taking his own.

He used to join in on roaming the streets, but the edges of the town were his home now, his sanctuary, and he balanced a crouch on his strong legs, his torso wrapped in sinewy muscle and tanned skin, his face rugged and sharp. He was beautiful.

All of his beasts were beautiful. It was their curse to be trapped in one land where the idea of mates was destined to be from only a handful of options.

The king inhaled once more, tingling with this new hunger inside of him. It was an urge to hunt, to find, yet he couldn't fathom its origin. He hadn't had an urge to roam the streets in a hundred years.

Yet on this night, he felt his muscles ripple, and his bones break, and when he stood on four legs and not two, he took off into the night.

Her phone woke her up.

It sang Beyonce, Charlotte's idea of a queen among all women. She felt numb like she'd been drugged and was pushing against its effects.

She hung upside down, the seatbelt bruising her shoulder and abdomen. In the way you would discover where you are after waking in a foreign place, she panicked.

The deer, the crash, the spinning and turning, and then blackness… it came rushing back to her, and she let out a slow, slow sob as the pain met her as well.

Her arm was wrong. It felt wrong, and it certainly looked wrong even in the darkness. Oh, god, the darkness.

Her phone stopped ringing, then picked up once again, and Charlotte realized with a vengeance just how terrible her situation really was.

The beasts. The beasts were roaming the streets.

Her car was upside down, and she fumbled with her seat belt, gasping in air that was hard to breathe in. When it released, she dropped to the hood of the car and let out a strangled scream, biting onto her good hand to muffle the sound.

The beasts were roaming.

She was panting and bleeding, but she didn't know from what wounds. She seemed to be bleeding from everywhere. She reached for her phone as it stopped ringing, and she cried out, distraught, as panic in its purest form seized her.

Charlotte was always on time you see. She did everything right, every damn thing, yet she crashed when others had practically given themselves to the beasts, and now… she'd be considered an offering, and *they* could drag her away with them.

She reached out with her good arm, across glass that bit her pale skin, and pulled herself forward. Her arm trembled, her side ached, and something in her leg felt off, but she pulled forward nonetheless, and when the upper half of her body was outside of the smashed window, she took a break before continuing. She knew she shouldn't, but she laid on her back anyways, staring up at the moon and those tiny, tiny stars when she was out of the car.

Her phone rang again.

She answered it quickly but found it hard to bring to her ear. "Charlie?" It was her mom crying. "Charlie, baby, where are you?"

How could she tell her? How could she tell her that she was done for? That she had crashed fifteen miles from the nearest shelter? She let the phone press into her shoulder while she regained her breathing and stopped tears she didn't know she was crying.

"The seminar ran late." She told her mom when she was sure she was able to speak. Her voice didn't sound like her own. It sounded distraught, broken, and laced with different flavors of pain. "I'm staying with a friend in Audet for the night."

"Charlie, you alright?" Her mom had stopped crying, but her voice was intuitive and nervous.

Again, she turned her face from the phone and bit her bloodied lip hard to stop from sobbing. She brought the phone back to her ear. "I'm fine, Mom. I promise."

She was bleeding, a lot, and she could see the dead deer a few feet away bleeding as well. How long before the beasts smell it? Smell her? Take her?

In the distance, she could hear the sound of rustling leaves and twigs snapping.

"Charlotte." Her mom's voice was low. "Charlotte, baby—"

"Mom." She cut her off because she knew her mom could read right through her. She was her mom, and for crying out loud if you couldn't tell Charlotte was in pain from her voice alone, you must've been daft. "I'm fine. I'll be fine."

"Oh, god." Her mom sobbed once more, strangled and pleading for her daughter's life. "Charlie—"

The rustling got louder, and before she could say I love you to her mom, her dad, her brother, or her asshole of a dog, she hung up because the last thing she would ever subject her mother to hearing is her last breaths while the beasts take her away.

She threw the phone back into the car and reached up with her good arm to haul herself to her feet. When they come, she would not be lying down as an offering. When they come, even if she lands only one kick, they would know she wasn't willing, and her death wasn't by her own choice.

It hurt worse than anything, and she choked out certain sounds she had never heard before. But she was standing, albeit crouching, on her own two feet, or really one since her ankle was busted — but she's up. Her head swam, and she faced the forest with her back to her beloved Ford.

With a start, a terrible realization, she remembered her grandmother's training, and she dipped her fingers into her blood and drew on her good hand as best as she can with her broken one.

Because maybe, in a town founded on magic and surrounded by monsters, she had a chance. Maybe those six years of training to learn these forsaken runes would be worth it.

Maybe, she had a chance.

She tracks the incoming sounds from the forest so closely that when a man stepped from the foliage, and not a beast, she nearly passes out. She's relieved, see, because it's a person and she'll be saved…

… if, say, that man was fully clothed, and if, say, he hadn't emerged from the very woods the beasts came from

Even as he stepped onto the road, she could see his jaw shifting from wide and pierced to that of a beautiful human jaw, his canines slipping from his lips, and his eyes striking and iridescently glowing.

He paused as he stepped onto the tarmac and breathed in deeply, those stunning eyes draping over Charlotte like no one else had.

The beast, she mused, *is human or pretends to be human.* She felt hot and in pain, and her head was swimming viscously from her blood loss as the man took another step… and another and another. He was running now, sprinting up the road from where he emerged and towards Charlotte as she swayed on her only good foot.

She held up her hand, the one she had managed to draw a protection symbol on, and gasped in agony as a spasm hit her spine and the man stopped in his tracks.

"No," he said, his eyes turning to slits as he saw the symbol. It was intricate, curling and looping, and it had to be perfect to work. But Charlotte loves to draw, and it took her six very, very long years to learn this one. "No."

From the woods, others emerged, but they were wolves, and these were the real beasts with lips pulled back, snarling. Her worst nightmare was presenting itself to her, but she was too far gone with the pain and the swimming of her head that she could hardly care. She sagged against the back of her car before letting herself drop down.

"Take it off." The man demanded as he came as close to her as the ward allowed him. It burnt his skin, making him feel woozy, but this was his life he was looking at now, broken and crumpled. This was his forever, and he couldn't even touch her to save her from dying. "Take it off!"

Charlotte smiled at this beautiful, beautiful stranger. "My grandma taught me this one." She gasped, closing her eyes so the snarling beasts around her won't be the last thing she remembers when she dies. "I went through training to learn it, so you can't fault her."

"You will die!" the man roared so loudly that the trees shuddered down to their roots. "Take it off!"

She felt how close he was, just inches from his bare skin, but he couldn't come closer. He couldn't bite into her neck and kill her or grab onto her and drag her away like a barbarian. When her mom finds her, she would be very much herself, very much in one piece… and very much dead against the side of her car.

"Does it upset you…" she whispers, "to not be able to take another one?"

The beasts snarled once more.

"Quiet," the man hisses, and the chorus around them was silenced. She opened her eyes, surprised at this display of authority. The beasts, in her mind, seemed like a bunch of lawless monsters. She met his blue eyes and the raw desperation within and watched him quickly scan the ground and splash his hand in a puddle of her blood. He was not touching her, but her blood.

"What are you doing?" she asked even as her vision clouded over. His hand ran over his bare chest, drawing deep red lines against pale white canvas. It was a symbol she could barely recognize. It was so familiar, yet she couldn't think clearly.

"Don't." She gasped, her surprise awakening her for a moment. She remembered the symbol now. "I'm not yours. You can't…"

It was a symbol used so a claimed one could touch what's theirs past any other symbol… even past her own personal rune etched into her palm with her own blood. That same blood, the only thing that could be used, was now splayed across the beast's chest.

His eyes met hers, a wild gleam in them, as he reached for her. "You will not die," he hisses. "You will be with me, always."

When he touched her skin, she sobbed. She was too far gone to feel *it* as the beast felt it. To him, it felt like everything he never had in his hundreds of years of life rested within the battered girl. Meanwhile, all she felt was a moment of utter loss as her last defense crumbled away. She didn't even feel the pain so much when he hauled her into his arms and walked back to the forest.

By then, she was already gone.

Chapter 3

She was not dead. She couldn't be. He had used the rune to touch her, to bring her back. She wasn't dead.

But the pack healer was shaking her head, tears welling in her eyes and falling down the lines of her old, aged face. People were grabbing onto him, the King of Beasts, holding onto his shoulders and muttering thing in his ear, but she wasn't dead.

What were they all so sad about when she couldn't be dead?

He pushed past everyone. They all crowded there when he fell in front of the healer's door, begging for the battered girl's life, panting from running so fast just to get her there. They had flocked around the old house and inside of it, in the small back room where the healer worked her magic. There were too many people.

He pushed the healer away as gently as he could in his desperation, his hands touching the bruised and swollen face of his mate. She wasn't dead. See, she just couldn't be. Her chest wasn't moving, sure, and he couldn't hear a heartbeat with those magnificent ears of his, but she wasn't dead. That would be impossible because he had waited two hundred years for her and all he got was a bloody symbol on his chest and her dying breaths while he held her, running through the woods.

She couldn't be dead.

He grabbed onto her shoulders, running his hands through that tangled mess of red hair on her head and wiping smears of blood from her cheek. A hand rested on his shoulder. It was his second in command talking to him, telling him he was so sorry, that they'd have a ceremony, and that it was a great loss for the whole pack. But then again, she wasn't dead.

The king snarled and threw his friend's hand from his shoulder. "She's not dead." He growled, standing to face the room. He was still naked and caked in dirt and his mate's blood. "She's not."

Odin shook his head sadly, reaching for him once more. "She's gone, Gabe. There's no getting her back."

"Out!" he roared because these were accursed words they were whispering. "Get out!"

He waited two hundred years, and if she was gone, if she had really died, then he couldn't... He couldn't even think.

God, she's gone, isn't she? he thought. *She is really gone.*

His shoulders shuddered violently, not his wolf but his human, trembling from the weight of it. Inside of him, that deep animalistic part that made it possible for him to find this wild-haired girl on that road by instinct was splitting in half and falling to pieces. Misery, pure and unrestrained, burned his insides, and Odin was there again, grabbing his shoulders.

They had never seen their king cry, and he didn't now. There was something too deep about this pain. It was too pure for the tears to mean anything. She was gone. She was really, really gone.

"We'll do a proper queen's burial," Odin muttered under his breath as their entire pack was shuddering, crying, and howling from the pain of their king and the pain of losing their new queen. "She was a part of us already, Gabe. We'll send her off like one."

He turned and fell to his knees by his girl... his beautiful, breathtaking girl, the only piece of himself that was missing. He only heard her voice, defiant and small, a brief enough encounter to know she was perfect. God, everything about her had been so perfect. She would've been the perfect queen, the perfect mate, and the perfect human to rule a pack of beasts.

But no longer. She wasn't here anymore. She couldn't feel his hand on her unbroken arm as his fingers brushed over her skin, stroking it, not believing how soft she was, how gone she was, and how quickly her skin was cooling.

There was nothing more... nothing more inside of him or before him, or anything else he could even think about. He just has his dead mate lying in the healer's room with his pack helplessly staring. God, their howls wasn't helping, an unbearable pain held in each ripping sound.

Suddenly, she sat up with her eyes opened, so green, so wide, and so alive. Her eyes were everywhere at once, and her heartbeat was roaring back to life. It was so loud in his ears, he could only stare back. The entire pack fell into silence as they felt life rush back into their pack just as it was restored into her body.

And then she started screaming.

Chapter 4

She was on the roof.

She couldn't exactly remember how she got up there. The past two days had been a blur of terror and confusion. Too many faces, too many people trying to touch her.

Yes, they were all people, not beasts. They smiled, had small, adorable children, and gave her gift baskets like they weren't beasts.

They had been so excited to see her, to say a few words while she stared wide-eyed with her heart in her throat and preparing herself for any one of these things to kill her in the back of her mind.

And that man… God, he never left her for even a second. His chair was pulled up beside her bed, and he tried touching her at first, just his hand on hers and his fingertips on her arm, but she swatted him away and cursed until her throat was raw. He was yelling at her not to curse, and she cursed him for telling her not to curse.

He was beautiful in an aching sort of way like if she looked at him for too long, she would just break. His dark hair was short and chopped, and his face was cut so clean with dark hairs rising up on his chin to his hairline. And his eyes... she had gotten too lost in them before. He'd say something, and she'd look at him without thinking because sometimes it felt natural to converse with him, to be so close to him and for him to touch her hand. His eyes would hold onto hers, and she would forget to breathe.

She liked the doctor, though. They called her a healer, and she was kind, old, and smarter than Charlotte could ever hope to be. She patched up her arm in a cast. When it was hurting unbearably, she could only close her eyes, grit her teeth, and ignore the man when he begged her to tell him what he could do to help. The healer put a salve into her cast, and she felt better.

Now, she was on the roof, and in the house and the fields surrounding the house, Charlotte could hear the commotion of her captors.

The man had gone to the bathroom, telling her before he left like he always did. Perhaps, he thought it would distress her to not know where he was. She hated that she would wake up sometimes and he wouldn't be in the room. She could feel the distress bloom in her stomach like she needed him in the room with her.

It's why she pulled herself up to her feet when he left on that second day even when her ankle screamed at her. It was why she shuffled to the window, pulled it open with one hand, and pulled herself out, sweating now because her body was screaming at her. Something in her side was ripping again. She closed the window behind her and took in a deep, deep breath of the cool morning air.

She was on the second floor of an old Victorian house, and there was another floor above hers. She was standing on a roof hanging over a large porch. Charlotte wasn't stupid enough to attempt escape. She had seen a hundred people come through to see her in the past two days, and from her perch on the roof, she could see the tiny, compact town bustling with people on the streets.

It was beautiful, a place cut out in the trees with dozens of old, magnificent houses. She could see kids chasing each other just like in her own town, parents chasing the kids, and men picking up their women and spinning them around even when the women were squealing.

They didn't act like a bunch of beasts.

And so, she couldn't escape, not with everyone everywhere, not with her ankle so busted, and not with only one good arm. However, she needed air, she needed to breathe, and that room wasn't allowing her that. She moved so her back wasn't to the window and sat down, laying her head against the rough tiling of the roof. She stared up at the sky, the clouds tinted a beautiful orange and pink from the sunrise.

It smelled wonderful out there.

She could hear the man when he came back to the room. She thought he would come straight to the window and drag her back in because, to her, it was obvious she had crawled out there, but he howled instead to Odin, a man she learned was some sort of a friend to him. She could hear them running through the house, screaming her name until their voices went hoarse, and then the whole town was calling for her. Queen, they called her. Did anyone know her name? No, she figured, because she hadn't told them, and she hung up on her mom before the beasts could hear her name.

She closed her eyes and breathed through her nose and out through her mouth so the pain was in the back of her head. She thought about quantum mechanics and the placement of electrons in their orbitals. She thought about the semi-permeable phospholipid bilayer of her cells and osmosis. She thought about her dog and how she would only sleep at the end of her bed, and how when she wasn't home, she would pace on the porch waiting for Charlie's return.

No one came looking for you when the beasts came. No one ventured into the woods to find their loved ones. It meant condemning the whole town, and if the officials thought you might go out for your daughter, sister, or mother, sometimes your father, brother, or son, then they would lock you up in the town jail cell until you calmed down and mourned like the rest of town for the lost life.

Because that's what Charlotte was now… a lost life.

"On the roof!" she heard someone say. She closed her eyes tighter, cursing under her breath because her thoughts were ruined. She heard a grunt, and she opened her eyes to see her very own stranger pulling himself onto the roof. Had he jumped up here? Dear lord!

"You scared the hell outta me." He panted, crawling towards her. She couldn't deny, no matter how she tried, that he was beautiful and perfect. She turned her head back so she was staring at the sky, and he came to a stop beside her. "Come on. I'll help you back inside."

"Just another moment," she whispered, her voice very quiet. "I like to watch the sunrise."

He paused, she could practically feel his conflict, before he moved and laid down beside her, their hands almost touching. She also couldn't deny that it had felt odd without him right beside her like he had been the past few days. It was a routine she had assumed. You live with something long enough, and it would be weird when it changes.

"You always watch the sunrise?" he asked her. His voice was deep when he wasn't yelling or commanding, rumbling from far within his chest.

She hummed in the back of her throat, watching the colors swirl and change above her. "I used to swim to it. I'd chase the colors across our lake."

They were silent again, and her body trembled with the pain of her small movements to get out there. She could hear people moving about below her, but she ignored them. She felt his fingertips touch the back of her hand, and she pulled it back so it laid across her stomach. "I won't hurt you," he muttered, angered again by her dismissal.

"I would like to go home, please," she said.

Another pause and she expected his answer. "You can't."

"You know, we all thought you killed the people you dragged away," Charlotte said, turning to look at the stranger beside her. His startling eyes met hers, taking away her breath.

He gave her a gentle smile that transformed his face into something more beautiful, more breathtaking. It almost hurt her eyes. "No one will ever hurt you."

She turned away. She had to. She got trapped when she stared at him for too long.

"Please don't run off like that again. You scared me," he said into the surrounding silence.

"The only reason I stopped at the roof is because I have a busted ankle." She shot back haughtily. She never knew how to hold her tongue, but she was grateful she didn't swear, too. He had told her enough times how he hated her cursing.

He growled, low in the back of his throat, reminding her of exactly what he was. A sliver of fear ran through her gut. "You can't leave. We're everywhere all the time. You'll only upset the others by leaving."

"Because I'm supposed to give up the feelings of my own family for those of yours? They think I'm dead, and you want me to stay here when I don't even know your damn name."

"Don't swear," he mumbled, but it was a second thought like he didn't have any conviction behind it anymore. "My name is Gabriel. You can call me Gabe."

And for some reason, after he had helped her back inside and the healer came and made her tired muscles and bones numb, she turned to Gabe and whispered quietly, "Charlotte."

After she tossed and turned for an hour, Charlotte always settled on her right side. He wasn't sure if it was because of her casted arm, but he thought it was perfect. He slept on his right side too, after all, and she was the perfect size to press right into his chest.

Charlotte was beautiful. Not like the beasts, but maybe that's why Gabe thought she was spectacular. She had eyes too wide for her face, hair too wild for her head, and a mouth too dirty for someone so perfect. The urge to touch her, to have any sort of contact with this beautiful human, was sometimes overpowering… so much that he would wait the entire day for her to close her eyes and drift away so he could grab onto her hand. In her sleep, Charlotte never fought him, and it was blissful peace for him. He would get scarce amounts of sleep just for a few more hours of waking attention to his beautiful, beautiful girl.

Primal urges to protect and possess would overwhelm the King of Beasts sometimes. She seemed so… fragile like if he looked at her for too long, she'd break. He found her crumbled and broken after all, and that seemed to be the way of humans. They are always breaking, always falling apart.

His Charlotte, though, was something special, something *too* special. Spoken in hushed whispers outside of her door, the healer expressed her age-old worries of the girl who came back to life. She was dead, the healer explained, dead for more than five minutes. Brain activity should've been minimal if alive at all. He didn't want to hear it. He didn't want to acknowledge that Charlotte had almost left him after he had just found her, but it was a strange phenomenon, one that made her interesting.

He sat in the dark now, chair pulled up to her bedside and fingers wrapped around her hand.

Charlotte had nightmares. Sometimes, she would tremble in her sleep, and he would watch, wondering if he should leave. Perhaps, his presence caused her to hurt, and that though hurt him, too. He would never want to leave Charlotte, never wanted to look anywhere but at her, and never wanted to feel anything other than the touch of her skin.

But eventually, after she would toss, turn, and tremble and then settle on her right side, he would succumb to the primitive urge to hold her, and he would grab her hand. Her tiny, fragile fingers would grip his with a ferocity that he was growing to absolutely admired in his tiny little mate. Her trembling would cease, her cries would quieten, and his beautiful, beautiful girl would fall into a deep sleep while clutching onto his hand like she would drown without it.

And for the first time in two hundred years, he hated the roaming of the beasts. He hated himself. God, he didn't even know what he hated. He just hated the fact that Charlotte had been here for four days, one of which she was dead for, another of which she had spent hours ceaseless cursing at him, and another where she escaped out a window to watch the sunrise. He hated that he had just found her, and she wanted to run already. He hated that he had to wait for her to settle on her right side before he could touch what he had been dreaming of holding for two hundred years.

The other humans had lasted a week before the pull overwhelmed them, and they succumbed. Besides, they were happy. Why couldn't Charlotte understand she would be happy, that Gabe would do anything he was capable of doing to give her what she wanted… that he would worship her as though she was a goddess created for him? She was his beautiful, perfect salvation, but she hated him.

No, it was worse. She *feared* him.

But in the dark hours of the night when she wasn't fighting the urge to touch him, when she wasn't cursing at him until it felt like his ears were bleeding, when she wasn't doodling periodic elements on scratch paper to ignore him, she gave into Gabe. She sighed when he touched her, a small puff of air escaping from her beautiful lips. Her muscles would relax. She would stop dreaming, and she would hold him back.

So he waited, sitting in his chair, and so did his pack. Everyone waited for their queen to come out and join them... for Charlotte to grab onto Gabe's hand when she was awake and sigh like she did when she was asleep.

Because maybe then, and only then, the beast wouldn't have to roam the streets any longer.

Chapter 5

One more branch, she told herself breathlessly, just one more branch. The twigs clawed at her skin, tearing through her soft, pale flesh. Her ankle was threatening to give out each time she hauled herself up, and her cast was torn and filled with leaves and foliage.

God, she was tired, a deep sort of tired. She had spent the past few hours limping her way into the shadows and darkness of the woods and then another hour drowning in her own panic.

What was happening to her?

She wrapped her good hand around the rough bark of a branch and pulled, her lungs aching and her muscles screaming. She felt incredibly stupid… stupid for crashing her damn car that night, stupid for just sitting in that healer's room and waiting for herself to heal enough to run. Stupid, *stupid*, Charlotte. She should have run the moment she had a chance.

Finally, only because she had no strength left in her tiny limbs, she rested herself on a thick branch with her back against the trunk of a sturdy oak. She was cocooned with branches, mostly hidden by leaves, and she closed her eyes tight when she had a moment.

The night was cold and bit at her torn up skin, making her crane up her neck to find the moon through the last few leaves above her. *Stupid.* God, she was so stupid... stupid for staying and even more stupid for running. How far had she gotten? A few miles? How had it taken her a few miles to realize she had no idea where she was in this forsaken forest? She felt like she was going to pass out.

Stupid, Charlotte. So, *so* stupid. Why did she have to just sit there, stare at him, and get lost in those blue eyes for the thousandth time? Why did he have to look so human? Why did he have to look... so beautiful?

Why did he have to kiss her like that?

And why did he have to look so distressed afterward and go roam the streets of her tiny little town just hours afterward and make it feel like he had somehow . . . betrayed her?

She stared up at the moon through the forest canopy, feeling lost and exhausted.

Gabe couldn't help it. The king of the beast, the man to rule them all, had lost control.

At first, he blamed her. After all, she stared at him with her wide, green eyes like she wanted him to touch her... like she was waiting for the touch of his lips on her. He had only meant to wake her up from her nap so she could eat, and she sat up in that tired way she does, rubbing her eyes and looking up at him. Then she just sat there, staring.

Maybe it was because he had just come back from a run, and his shirt was thrown on the front porch drenched in sweat. Maybe it was because she had not seen his bare chest since the night Gabe had found her, but even then, it was covered in her blood.

He shook his head, growling low at himself.

He had lost control.

There seemed to be no reason not to take three long strides across the room and bend down so one hand was on the bed beside her hip and the other was brushing across her cheek, listening to the sound of her soft gasp and feeling the way his hand zapped with some sort of intense electricity. She didn't give him any reason to stop himself from lowering his head and brushing his lips across her cheek. So soft, she had been so soft.

She practically asked him to kiss her, didn't she? The way her eyes fluttered close so her eyelashes hit his cheeks, and the way she sighed against him... she basically asked him, right?

She tasted like peanut butter. When the hell had she eaten peanut butter? Her good hand reached up and touched the side of his face, her fingers trembling as they ran down his jaw line. She felt so good. God, she felt like two hundred years' worth the wait.

He admitted, standing on the outskirts of her town where he used to perch each and every night, that he shouldn't have done it when he had listened to her for two hours as she cursed him out and his entire beastly town the day before.

He might have lost control.

He had waited so long for her, and he and his wolf couldn't help it. He couldn't help it.

She slapped him, sure, and that was rough. And she stood up even after she cried out in pain from her leg and then limped to the opposite corner, pointing her finger at him and screaming at him to leave. *Get out! Who the hell did you think you are?* she said.

What else could he do but run? His mate, that perfect human being, was terrified of him and rejected him. She didn't want him. She didn't want him near her, and he got angry. Angry because... damn it, he didn't even know why. He just felt somewhere deep inside that she had hit him hard, and he wanted nothing more than to lock her in a closet until she had no choice but to accept him.

Maybe he thought coming out here would put normalcy back into his life. Perhaps, it would calm him down. Yet it did the exact opposite. He stood in the trees and listened as a wolf howled in victory. Another mate. Odd, considering just a few weeks ago he had another pack mate found his own mate. That was. . close.

He stood there for an hour before his wolf ripped through. He then paced there, still trying to regain control, before he lost it for the second time that day.

He didn't care if Charlotte didn't want to see him or if she was scared of him. She had kissed him back, damn it, and that stubborn girl was going to see him even if she didn't want to. She was his mate, and she needed to realize it. She needed to accept it.

No... No, she didn't need to. She was perfect, and she could take all the time she needed. He just — needed to touch her. He just wanted to hold her hand while she slept on her right side because she never slapped him and ran away from him then.

God, what was he doing?

What the hell was Charlotte doing to him?

He shifted mid-step as he got to the healer's home. It was late, and the old healer was asleep. He had kept some clothes in her living room since Charlotte was staying here, and he threw a pair of shorts on before bounding up the stairs, slowing outside of her door so he wouldn't wake her.

He would talk to her in the morning. He would explain himself to her. He had to explain everything as best as he could, and then he wouldn't lose control ever again. He would wait another two hundred years if he had to for her to realize that Gabe would be with her forever, would do anything she ever wanted. Maybe then she would be the one to lose control and go to him.

But when he opened her door quietly, he only saw an empty bed. The blankets were thrown back, her crutches missing, and the stale scent of her on the sheets saying she had not been there for hours.

He blinked, slowly, staring at her sheets for longer than necessary as though she would magically show up.

The next moment, he was running faster than he ever had, entering the forest where he could smell her panic and her fear, and followed it like he would break apart if he didn't. That was certainly how he felt, though.

Chapter 6

There was an animal beneath her.

It was big, and loud, and didn't hide the fact that it had her scent and was circling the oak Charlotte perched on. Gabe? No, she figured when Gabe found her he would be a mess of fury and claws and snarling. This animal seemed... curious.

She tried peering down through the foliage, but in her attempt to hide herself from below, she had effectively hidden everything from above, too. She listened, ever so carefully, to the breaking of twigs and the deep inhalations of the animal before a horrendous sound seemed to fill the night air.

Cracking, breaking, tearing, and then a man panting heavily at the end of it.

Charlotte brought her fist to her mouth and bit down hard to stop herself from crying out in panic. It was one thing to be trapped in a town of beasts, and it was another thing to be subjected to their change.

"Come here, girly," a stranger's voice whispered. "Come here girly girly girly. I can smell you. Mmm, I can smell you alright. You smell like Alpha. You smell like strong Alpha."

Alpha? What in the holy hell was an alpha? She thought. His voice was deep, grave, and had that thin lining of insanity around its edges. If this beast knew how to climb a tree, then she would be fu—

He was climbing the tree.

Charlotte looked around herself wildly, her reddish orange hair catching the moonlight and glowing like embers. There was nowhere to go. Well, she did not really think when she climbed this tree. She was tired from all the running, and she was terrified that if she rested on the forest floor, the beasts would catch her while she napped.

It seemed safest to get up high, but she never really thought about the fact that the beasts were human, too, and humans could climb. She could hear him grunting as he climbed up, and Charlotte cursed, swinging her legs over to the other side of her branch.

"Come here, girly. I won't bite." She heard him pause then a deep, maniacal laugh. "Well, I guess I might. You smell mighty fine, girly. What nice old alpha let you roam out on our own?"

She couldn't very well jump to another tree, could she? Certainly, she would fall, and she was high enough for it to be fatal. Her only option, then, was to descend on the other side of the tree and hope she was low enough by the time her and the beast's path intercept so she could jump.

Where would she run to, though?

"Good girly, coming down to meet me," the beast hummed, his voice greedy and crazed. "Girly going to be a good girly. Why do you smell like strong alpha, girly? Where's your strong alpha?"

She hung from one branch with one hand until her good ankle rested on a branch below. She hooked her cast across a sturdy setting and then lowered herself carefully. When she heard the beast shifting to come up the same side of the oak she was descending, she also shifted so they were always opposite.

"Strong alpha..." the beast said again, although his voice was more unsure and confused. "Strong, *strong* alpha. Strongest alpha." He grunted, then climbed up again. Charlotte heard a new fervor in his advances, and she felt like screaming for Gabe. She wanted Gabe right now. Not her mom, her dad, or anyone from town but the beast that had stolen her.

Finally, when she didn't expect, his face came from behind the trunk just inches from her. A startled scream escaped her lips. He was ragged and dirty, and his breath smelled like death and blood. His teeth were crooked and chipped, and some were definitely missing. Scars ran down his face and the length of his naked, gnarled body. Charlotte gagged.

"Hey there, girly," he said, flashing her a toothy grin. "You're a pretty girly."

He reached for her, and she let herself drop. Her good ankle slipped from the branch below her, and she fell a good foot before her good hand found another branch to grab onto. Gasping, heart beating wildly, thoughts all but nonexistent, she continued her decent although now it was more falling than anything else.

"Girly, I thought you were a good girly!" the beast called, his voice insane and angry. "You smell like good strong alpha, girly. You should be good!"

She couldn't curse or swear at anyone but herself as a new type of fear ate her inside out. Gabe had never hurt her. He had saved her, actually, and the other beasts had equally done no harm. But this beast, the one coming after her… She didn't even want to imagine what he had planned for her.

The ground was close now, almost close enough to drop to, but when she was releasing the old branch above her head, she felt a surprisingly strong fist wrap around her wrist. Startled, she glanced up at the beast.

"Gotcha, girly." He grinned.

Charlotte screamed, and from below them, a ferocious, earth-shattering, bone-breaking growl threatened to tear the night in half.

Charlotte grinned almost as insanely as the man whose face had suddenly turned terrified. The king of the beasts had arrived. He was here for his queen, and for once, Charlotte was okay with that.

Chapter 7

There was fury like nothing he had felt before burning through Gabe's limbs. Just the sight and the mere thought of that rogue touching what was his made him want to kill. He wanted to kill the rogue... to kill anyone who ever touched *his* Charlotte.

He shifted as he came to a halt at the base of the tree, standing tall and breathing deeply. His Charlotte was dangling twenty feet in the air, her eyes wide and staring from Gabe to the man holding her. "Release her," Gabe growled, the beast in him writhing to climb the tree and tear that rogue limb from limb, "NOW!"

The authority in his voice had every wolf within ten miles trembling and falling to their knees in submission, and the rogue was no exception. Whimpering like a wounded animal, he immediately released Charlotte, and she fell. A scream seemed to lodge itself in her throat, and she crashed through the last branches, plummeting to the forest floor.

Gabe caught her easily, making sure her ankle and arm were unharmed. He pulled her as close to him as he could manage. She was trembling. His little, always fierce Charlotte was trembling. What number had the rogue done to her to make her unable to fight Gab even when he held her so close?

"I'm going to put you down now," Gabe said quietly, trying to contain his voice so it was soothing to not startle Charlotte any further. She tensed in his arms for a moment, her hands gripping his biceps like she wasn't going to let go, before she thought better of it and released him.

He set her down at the base of an opposite tree and then faced the rogue as he descended rapidly, trying to flee before the king of beasts could stop him. "Cepheus." Gabe snarled, and the rogue flinched as though the man had hit him. "I thought I told you to get off my land."

The rogue nodded rapidly with his head bent, his naked body heaving with vicious breaths. "I did, I did, I *did*. I smelled girly, though. She smells good."

Gabriel snarled and advanced toward the poor rogue. Charlotte was his. Charlotte belonged to him. Not this piece of filth or anyone else.

The rogue trembled, but there was no escape. Not from the king of beasts, not when that animalistic side of him had taken control wanted death. The rogue knew it was best to stand still and wait.

"Gabe." Her small voice was tight and nervous, yet it spoke through the murderous fog in his head the way only she could. She reached out right to the center of him, right to that piece only she owned, and had him stopping in his tracks and turning to her. Something in his gaze must have been feral because his little mate flinched back from him.

She swallowed to gain some resolve and met his ferocious gaze. "Don't, please. I want to go back."

Don't kill the rogue? He thought.

There were plenty of things Gabe would do for his mate and plenty of things he would let her ask him. This was not one of them. Cepheus had touched her, planned to defile her, and planned to kill her or take her away. Well, hell, it didn't matter. He had to *die.*

Gabe snarled and turned back to the rogue, pacing closer, fingers twitching and elongating into claws for a swift kill.

"Gabriel…"

His shoulders rode up to his ears, and he stood still mere feet from the trembling, submissive rogue. Like he was fighting through cement, he turned his head back to look at Charlotte.

"I will never look at you the same if you do this. I want to go back."

She found a weak spot, *again.* Wounded, his beast whimpering, Gabe was hopeless. Now he couldn't kill the rogue, not like he needed to. He wanted to. His little mate ensured that. She was scared, though. She was curled up against the tree, hugging her knees in the dark and cold, her green eyes wide and terrified, and looking at Gabe like she thought he was everything.

Damn it.

He turned back to the rogue and snarled, the sound ripping from his throat and making the other beast whimper.

"You will leave," Gabe commanded. He could feel the power dripping from his voice, settling into the soil so even the trees fought their roots not to run. "You will *never* come back. If you do, I will kill you. Not even my mate will stop that. Leave!"

And he did, scampering away into the night. Gabe shifted when he was out of sight and running wild. He turned back to Charlotte when he was sure the malice was cleared from his thoughts. She didn't flinch when he approached her, but she did look away. He assumed it was because he was naked, and the humans were always more clothed than him and his beasts.

He crouched beside her, unable to stop himself from running his fingers over her soft, pale cheek to feel her and know she was here and she was his. She didn't flinch from his touch, either... not until his fingers lingered a moment too long, and she pulled away from him.

She didn't flinch, though, and Gabe took that as a win.

"Let's go back," he said, taking her hand and pulling her to her feet. "I'll carry you—"

"I can walk." She cut him off, limping in front of him. He grabbed onto her hand, and before she could protest, he turned her in the right direction and let her and her wounded pride limp onwards. "And you can't kiss me like you did earlier or touch me like that. I- I won't allow it."

Even he could hear the uncertainty in her voice, and he allowed himself to smile quietly as he followed her from behind. "I will not kiss you like that our touch you like that again." He assured her and watched her shoulders sag in relief. "Not until you want me to."

He could see the way her irritation spiked, but something about knowing exactly what to say to make her react a certain way was thrilling to him. He was figuring his Charlotte out, piece by hidden piece, and it was exhilarating.

Chapter 8

Safe. She was safe. She had some minor cuts and bruises, and she smelled like stale sweat, the forest, and that rogue, but she was safe.

It was overpowering, almost all-consuming, the urge to bite her and mark her as his own. No damn rogue would dare come to her, their queen, again. She would be his... all his, safe and protected. But damn Charlotte for turning the king of beasts more human. He could not bite her, not until she asks him to.

He would make damn sure she asked him to.

They sat across from each other now, the small wooden table in his kitchen serving as their only barrier. He had insisted they go to the healer, that even though he could smell no damage, she might be hurt. Who knew what the hell that rogue had done to her? He should have killed the maniac who dared touch what was his.

He should have killed the damn rogue.

But Charlotte wanted to talk. She insisted and demanded. She didn't want to go to the healer so the old woman could give her a nice salve and some medicine that would make her sleep. She wanted to talk to Gabe and have a good, un-beastly conversation.

Her hands rested atop a table, folded together, as she assessed him. Gabe was a man who never lacked confidence. It was not in his genes to do so, yet when Charlotte looked at him like that, he felt like everything about him was wrong... that he should be better, leaner, stronger, and faster for her.

He reached forward, trying to be inconspicuous but needing to touch her again. The urges were getting more profound, more dominant. Maybe he thought she wouldn't notice him brush a finger over her knuckles, but she was pulling back before his hand had reached halfway across the table.

"Okay, that," she said, the first words they had spoken since she had cleaned up and limped back to his kitchen table. She was yet to comment on the fact that she was at Gabe's house, on uncharted territory. "That's what I want to talk about. You always touching me. It's — creepy," she said although he knew she was lying, could taste it in the air.

She wanted to touch him as badly as Gabe needed to touch her. It was the only way to appease his beast. "I want to touch you." He shrugged that massive shoulders of his. "It's quite simple."

Charlotte pursed her lips. "Th-that beast in the woods, he said something about an alpha."

Gabe stiffened. He had not been expecting a conversation like this so soon. He had not even thought about it, thought about his ranking, of being king of the beasts and what that would mean for Charlotte. He just wanted her to not hate him so bad.

"What's an alpha?"

He squared his shoulders and ran through the possible explanations in his head. "It's a leader," he said, settling lamely.

"He said you were a strong alpha… alpha of alphas."

God, his little red-headed beauty missed nothing, did she? "You hear what they call you," Gabe uttered, "the pack members."

"Pack members? You mean the townspeople? Yeah, they call me queen. I don't… I mean, I just don't get it. It's an odd title."

"I'm the alpha of alphas," Gabe said. His beast howled in agreement, threatening to break free and show his little spitfire just how much of an alpha he was. "I'm the king of beasts."

"And I'm…?"

Gabe lifted a perfect eyebrow, a look that had Charlotte squirming in her seat for some reason. Gabe had that uncanny ability to make her feel so much. "And you're my queen."

He watched her carefully, the way the blood drained from her face and the way her mouth went slack. He worried briefly if she had passed out before the color returned and Charlotte was on her feet, that annoyingly persistent fire burning within her once more.

"Like hell I am!" she cried, waving her casted arm. "I'm not a beast. I break. I die. I don't go around stealing kids from other towns and then pronouncing them as queen or king or whatever the hell you want to call it!"

Gabe calmed his innermost beast from clawing to the surface. He never had to calm himself. If he was angry, it was with reason. If his beast wanted to show dominance, it was deserved. He never needed a lesson in self-control, not until Charlotte walked into his life and pressed all of his buttons.

He rose slowly to his full height, his beautiful eyes piercing Charlotte. She cowered back from him, and the human within him hated that. Charlotte should never have to fear him even when his beast was howling with the submission.

"You know your runes." Gabe explained carefully. He didn't miss how her eyes were trained anywhere but on him and his bare chest. He had grabbed shorts off of his living room couch before joining Charlotte in the kitchen. He enjoyed how he affected her. "You know why I was able to break the one you had on your hand that night."

Charlotte winced and took a step back further into the kitchen so she hit the island and jumped. "Th-that... you... well, yeah. I mean, yeah... I know what you did." She huffed, her face flushing. "It was a claiming rune."

He waited for her to connect the dots. If there was one thing Gabe was absolutely certain about his Charlotte, it was that she was far smarter than he could ever be. When she did not seem to understand, Gabe sighed. She obviously did not want to know.

"It worked because I've already claimed you. The day I was born, you were claimed to be mine."

He watched the feminist inside her claw its way to the surface and waited patiently for the outburst, finding he thoroughly enjoyed his arguments with the little spitfire. She stirred something in his chest, emotions he hadn't felt in so long.

"You have no claim over me!" she exclaimed, moving around the island now so it separated her and Gabe. "I'm my own person, damn it!"

She was breathing heavily, eyes darting everywhere like she was looking for an escape.

"You are mine," he stated evenly, bristling at the way she ran from him like he was going to hurt her. "Your town was cursed long ago. A member of your town belongs to each member of my pack. It was destined a long time ago."

She shook her head, staring at Gabe like he was a bomb. "No," she said defiantly. Gabe felt a twinge of annoyance and anger. She was his, damn it. "I'm going home. I *will* go home, and you're going to let me."

"I can't do that," Gabe admitted, shaking his head. "I can't let you go."

So she ran, again. Even though he had just saved her an hour ago from her previous escape attempt, she ran. Limping with the brace on her ankle, she scrambled down the front hall to the door.

Something in Gabe seemed to snap. He swore he could hear the breaking in his ears. He was more beast than man, after all, and Charlotte was running again. When would she learn? When would she realize that her place was by Gabe, and that damn it, he wasn't going to hurt her!

"Charlotte, stop!" he roared, his voice pitched into his alpha command. It startled him, the level of authority and anger in his voice, and made the house shake in its frame. He heard her stumble to a halt in the hallway, and when he moved so he could see her, her shoulders were hunched up, and her body was tense. "Come back here."

She turned as though fighting a current. The look on her face was filled with so much rage and fear it seemed to punch Gabe in the stomach. Like she was walking through tar, Charlotte came back. He felt his control over her snap when she was feet away, and she let out a shuddering breath.

"Never do that to me again." She threatened in a low voice, her hands shaking at her side as her pride shattered within her.

"Stop running from me, then," Gabe countered.

"I won't stop running!" Charlotte shouted, her face turning as red as her hair. "Don't you get that? You kidnapped me, I'm always going to—"

Gabe lost control again. He just needed her to stop saying that she was going to run. He just wanted her to stay with him, to stop acting as though Gabe was going to hurt her, and to look at him with anything other than hate.

He was not sure why or how, but Charlotte was suddenly pressed into the wall with her good hand clutched to his chest and his lips molded perfectly against hers. For the first time, Charlotte didn't fight him.

Chapter 9

Gabe would not stop grinning. The man had practically assaulted Charlotte, and he was grinning.

Charlotte regarded him from afar as he was talking to the townspeople. Even the red mark on his cheek from where she slapped him had faded. Now, he was just a grinning idiot in a sea of beasts.

Charlotte rested on a high roof, the black tiles burning the backs of her legs. She wondered if she was developing a fetish for roofs, then snorted. She had been wandering aimlessly through town and spotted the terribly installed solar panels. Her favorite lecture in the entire world was when the visiting professor came to her class and discussed solar panels. They were fascinating to her.

So she had broken into the house when no one answered the door, broke into the garage to steal some tools, then climbed up the stairs and out the window on the second floor. She was getting good at walking without crutches, and although her arm was still a hindrance, things were healing nicely.

She had been gone for about fifteen minutes now, and she wondered when Gabe would notice. He had been in a deep discussion when she had left. At first, she had wandered through the fresh foods market and ate an apple. When he didn't come after her, Charlotte just sort of... slipped away.

Her head was in a different place, had been since Gabe kissed her the other night. It felt right. It had felt normal, and it took her longer than it should have to push him away. It didn't feel like a first kiss. It felt like the thousandth kiss, like they have been touching each other their whole lives, like they knew everything about each other. It had been beyond perfect, beyond normal, beyond right.

Charlotte dropped the wrench back to the toolbox and rubbed a hand down her sweating face. It was hot out today, and the heat wasn't distracting her from her thoughts. Claimed? Could she really have been claimed by Gabe?

Her eyes found him amidst a group of men. He was handsome, terribly so. Maybe not conventionally, but to Charlotte, every piece of him was perfect... even the slight crookedness to his nose, even the way his chin was a bit too sharp, and even that glow in his eyes. He was perfect, and Charlotte swore under her breath because of it.

How could the elders of her town not tell her about this? They taught her runes. All of them trusted her greatly. They told her she would do important things, and they raised Charlotte like she was their own child. They said that one day she may be an elder, that she had the power for it, yet they didn't entrust her with this information. They let her believe, just like her whole town, that the beasts came, the beasts took, and the beasts killed.

As if sensing her eyes, Gabe looked up, caught mid-laugh so a smile was frozen. Gabe saw Charlotte a few streets away on the roof of a house much taller than the others. His head cocked to the side, confused, while other faces followed his line of sight. She watched him mouth her name, then his eyes widened in surprise and fear before he took off to the streets.

Charlotte rolled her eyes.

Stupid claiming, she thought. *That is so barbaric. What happened to women's rights? Didn't destiny understand the importance of feminism?*

"Charlotte!" she heard Gabe shouting, running toward her much faster than anyone should be able to run. "Are you alright? What the hell are you doing up there?"

"I'm plotting my death, Gabe," Charlotte replied dryly. She expected a haughty retort, and when she got none, she glanced at the ground warily. "Gabe?"

Arms were wrapped around her from behind, and she screamed, fearing for her balance and the ground below. She knew it was Gabe that had her, his touch she memorized, and she let out a shaky breath. "I was kidding!" she cried, slapping his arms.

Gabe growled and pulled her back along the roof. "Wait!" She gasped. "Wait — the panels! Damn it, Gabe, if you don't put me down I'll—I'll kiss you again!"

Gabe froze, a surprised laugh escaping his mouth. "So I should keep holding you?"

"I thought you'd be surprised and let me go," Charlotte admitted weakly.

Gabe did, although carefully, and turned Charlotte to face him. His hand brushed over her cheek, and she trembled although she told herself a breeze just passed by. "Your cheeks are burned," Gabe muttered disapprovingly.

"Stop touching me," she argued but didn't slap his hand away. "I understand the whole claiming thing. Sure, fine, but I'm not okay with it."

He pulled his hand back, nodding solemnly. "I would never force you to do anything."

She took a step back, swayed on the slant of the roof, and Gabe steadied her. "What did I say about touching?"

"Fine, I'll just let you fall off the roof next time," he said with a smile.

Charlotte swallowed, wondering how exactly this whole claiming thing worked and how it made her heart race when he smiled at her like that. "I've got to fix the panels," she muttered, turning and limping back. Gabe followed closely in case she slipped.

"How'd you get up here and why? You're always on a damn roof of all places."

Charlotte grinned and knelt down once more, retrieving the tools. "I broke into the house," she admitted coyly, feeling somewhat bad, but she was about to give this house a boost of energy, so she figured it was fine.

"And the tools?"

"I broke into their garage, too."

A silence enveloped them before Gabe laughed once more and sat beside her. "I didn't know you knew how to do this."

Charlotte shrugged. "I love this kind of thing. Energy was my passion."

She could feel his eyes on her, yet tried to ignore it. "I'm sorry I kissed you," he said after a long pause.

Charlotte nearly dropped her wrench but fought to keep a hold of it and to not look at Gabe. Once she looks into his eyes, she would be gone. "It's stupid to be predetermined to be with someone, get stolen away, and then have no choice but to fall in love with your captor just because your town was cursed. I like my choices, Gabe, and right now, I have absolutely none."

Another long silence. Charlotte was blushing, but she didn't know why.

"I'm sorry," he muttered again.

Charlotte cursed under her breath before turning and facing Gabe. "Look, I want to know the details, okay? I want an honest discussion. I want to know what the hell is going on between you guys and my town, why it was cursed, and what you expect from me. I'm not just going to sit here all docile and whatnot."

Gabe paused for a moment then nodded. "Fine. Then I want to know why the elders taught you those runes."

Charlotte was taken aback. She was not expecting that question. "B-because," she stuttered, "I'm good at them."

Gabe narrowed his eyes. "We'll talk when you're done."

Charlotte nodded carefully, her eyes guarded. "Fine."

She went back to work.

"Can I kiss you again?"

He laughed when he dodged the wrench thrown at his head, then sulked when Charlotte forced him to go retrieve it. Damn Gabe and the way she made Charlotte believe he was alright. Damn him and his laugh and his smile and that fine, fine ass of his as he walked back along the roof.

Charlotte cursed herself, then stared at her hands. How the hell was she supposed to figure anything out when all she wanted was for Gabe to stop asking if he could kiss her and just do it again? She shook her head, and because she was on a cursing roll, she cursed the claiming once more.

Chapter 10

She sits across from Gabe quietly. She was so passive, he can't read anything from her. Not a single twitch, not a single inclination of the head, not a single clue as to what was happening in that fantastic head of hers.

It was incredibly disarming.

"So," she said slowly, biting on her bottom lip in deep thought, "you're telling me that you're two hundred years old?"

Gabe nodded. He knew age was a problem with humans, but he also figured that after about a hundred year age gap, it didn't really matter anymore. Did it matter to his Charlotte? "I was born in 1807."

"So *over* two hundred." She corrects, but her voice is so monotonous that Gabe can't tell if that's a bad thing or a good thing, or if she even cares at all. Gabe personally feels like a thousand years old, feels like every memory carries the weight of a thousand without Charlotte by his side. She can keep him grounded now and stabilize him in a way he hadn't had before.

"And you are twenty," Gabe says because maybe she just wants to talk about numbers, maybe she doesn't care that Gabe is older... way older, past the point of robbing the cradle, past the point of conviction, and past any sort of point, really.

"Twenty-one in two weeks," she says absentmindedly. She was staring intently at Gabe now, eyes squinting, like she was trying to find a gray hair on his head. "You don't look a day over one fifty," she finally says.

It took Gabe one, two moments to figure out she was joking before a grin broke across his face. "Why, that's the nicest thing anyone has said to me in a century."

She was grinning now, too, and that was an accomplishment that made Gabe concerned. Why did he feel like she gives him the world every time she smiles at him like that... like she doesn't hate him? "Alright, so let's cut to it then." She clears her throat and sits up straighter. "What's the deal with you and my town?"

They were sitting in Gabe's kitchen once more, and Charlotte was yet to comment on the fact that they were not staying in his house. Again, he couldn't tell if that was a good thing or not. Women were confusing, and Charlotte was the most confusing of them all.

Gabe licked his lip nervously, trying to find some way to explain. In his town, this story was just known. The parents tell the kids, and the story just follows. Gabe never had to explain it to anyone before. Usually, that job was already done when he comes around.

"Your town is on an energy fault line," he started, and when Charlotte perked up, he figured he was saying something right, "and your elders settled there. Unfortunately, energy faults are binding. My great grandfather bound my pack to this land hundreds of years ago, hundreds before you. Our original pack broke into smaller ones, but they all remained here, bound to this area and unable to leave, or for others to enter."

He paused, but when Charlotte nodded eagerly for him to continue, he was helpless to do so. "Our women only give birth to males, though, and our women were dying. We couldn't leave to find the mates of our men, and women couldn't enter to become the mates of our men. Then your ancestors arrived, having searched for the fault line, and they and my grandfather settled an agreement."

Charlotte raised an eyebrow. "Let me guess," she said, bitterness lined in her voice. "They can stay as long as the women go with the men if a mate is found?"

Gabe hesitated and then nodded, knowing this would upset Charlotte. Which it did. He watched her face heat up in anger and prepared himself for an argument. "They agreed. They needed the fault line to survive, and we needed their women to survive."

Charlotte pulled a face that Gabe couldn't decipher, but he knew, at the very least, it wasn't good. "Oh, my god. I'm a breeding machine to you? That's what all the women are? Oh, god! Oh, my god! I'm not going to—you—I…"

"No!" Gabe said quickly, catching on to her line of thinking quickly. "No, you are my life. You are our lives. You are everything. Without you, there is no us. We have purposes in our lives, clear defined paths, and they always lead to our mates. There is no other reason for anything without you."

He had laid it on thick, but by the dazed look Charlotte was giving him, it had been just right. "That's... intense," she muttered, blushing.

Gabe grinned. She hadn't run screaming yet, and he would take that as a victory any day. "That's why we roam the streets."

She tucked red hair behind her ear before meeting Gabe's eye. "You said that we can't leave? That we can't leave the town? Or the area, I guess."

Gabe nodded. "Once you bind yourself to the area, you can never leave."

She raised a challenging eyebrow. "The elders leave all the time."

"That's because they're the elders. They can leave as they please." Upon her exasperated look, Gabe continued. "Your elders settled here with other peplum, but only the elders could use the energy from the fault line. It's in their genes, an ability, a species of their own. They can come and go as they please, but their settlers cannot."

"I left," she counters. "I went to the community college a few towns over. I was always running errands for my grandma."

Gabe felt the blood in his veins freeze, but he was careful, so very, very careful to not let anything show on his face. His Charlotte had been very good with her runes, and that spoke volumes on its own, but Gabe had been hoping that it was just from the thin traces of her lineage running through her veins. But if she could leave and not be affected by it, it meant much, much more.

"You're an exception."

"Gabe—"

"Did any of your classmates go to the community college?" Gabe cut her off. She shook her head slowly. "Did any of the kids go to college at all? Did they even want to? Did anyone in that town ever want to leave for any reason? Maybe to go to a new restaurant a town over, to see a new movie, to just leave and see something new? Ever?"

She did not respond, but he could see the slight tinge of understanding and fear in her eyes. "That's still so twisted," she muttered, looking at the table. "That because my ancestors a few hundred years ago signed an agreement that we all still have to bear the brunt of it."

Did she not know? Gabe tilted his head to the side, regarding Charlotte carefully before deciding she was genuine. "The elders, *your* elders, are the originals," Gabe said carefully. "They're not your ancestors yet."

She surprised Gabe by laughing. "My grandma is an elder." She giggled. "She's not two hundred years old."

Gabe raised an eyebrow. "What's her name?"

"Barbara."

"Barbara Strite?"

Charlotte froze, her eyes hardening. "How'd you know that?"

"Because she's the one that signed the contract."

Chapter 11

For Gabe's sake, he hadn't said anything. He hadn't really moved. Charlotte was thankful for that small miracle as she paced the lawn in his backyard. They had moved there when it felt like Charlotte was about to suffocate in his kitchen. The sun was warm, the air was cool, and Gabe looked delectable just lounging in his chair while Charlotte tried to not lose her mind.

"Okay, stand up," Charlotte announced suddenly, startling Gabe from his silent appraisal of Charlotte. "I want to test this thing, so stand up."

Cautiously, Gabe stood to his full, towering height. Beneath his flannel shirt, Charlotte could imagine the muscles rippling, the same muscles she had seen the first night she met him. She fought the blush when she thought of his naked body.

"Test what?" Gabe asked.

Charlotte waved a hand between the ten-foot space between them. "*This*. This whole mate thing. I can't just take your word for it."

"The rune—"

"The rune can be used on anyone," Charlotte cut him off harshly. "If you use enough power, any rune can be used on any person. Just because you used a claiming rune, doesn't mean I've claimed you back."

Gabe made a face as though he were about to argue before a serene look crossed his face, causing a shiver to run up Charlotte's spine. "Fine. Test it if you must."

"Take your shirt off." She demanded. Gabe lifted an eyebrow but did as she asked. Trying her best to remain impartial to all that man standing before her, she stepped close.

"Stay here," she muttered, brushing past him and back into the house. She shuffled around the island in the center and grabbed a knife from the block before going back out to the lawn. Gabe eyed the knife warily but said nothing. "I need your hand."

He offered his hand and didn't flinch when Charlotte drew the blade over the thin skin of his palm. Blood pooled on the small cut, and she tucked the knife into her pocket before touching his blood with her fingertips. Because she worked with runes since she was a child, this part of the process did not gross her out although Gabe's stare was nearly burning her.

"Should I be concerned?" he finally muttered.

Charlotte paused, her blood coated fingers inches from the solid muscles in his chest. "You should be fine. You might feel a burning sensation. There's a chance I could lose your soul, but I wouldn't worry."

She saw him stiffen but continued anyways, drawing quickly on his chest in elegant lines, perfectly executed despite the crude drawing material. She finished quickly and stepped back, admiring her work. Gabe lowered his chin to his chest right above the drawing, trying to see it. "What's it do?"

Charlotte didn't answer and instead, pulled the knife from her pocket and sliced her own palm. Where Gabe had been quiet when it was his turn, he shouted as Charlotte drew her own blood, snatching the knife away quickly. "Jesus, Charlotte!" he shouted, reaching to grab her hand like he was going to check on the wound.

Charlotte laughed and pulled her hand back, grinning at Gabe's outburst. "It's a small cut, smaller than yours. I'm fine."

She spread the blood on her palm then paused once more. "What?" Gabe asked, sensing her hesitancy.

Charlotte grimaced. "If you're lying, I swear I'll burn your house down," she said, meeting his eyes steadily.

The corner of his mouth turned up. "I can't lie to you, Charlotte. I'll never be able to lie to you."

She lowered her gaze to the symbol on his chest, took a deep breath, then slapped her bleeding palm on top of the rune.

Charlotte realized several things at once.

First, that she had never felt more powerful than she was the moment she touched Gabe. Even when she released his rune, that power still surged, making her hair stand on end.

Second, that Gabe's hair was softer than she could ever have imaged. It was like silk running through her fingers.

And third, that she was certain she had never felt anything better than what she felt when she was kissing Gabe.

His hands were on her hips, holding her so tight that she was sure there would be bruises there later. There was an overwhelming sense of belonging, of being at the most perfect spot in the entire world in Gabe's arms. Her back was pressed against the railing of his back porch, his lips hot and kneading against her own.

She could still feel his soul coursing through her hand and up her arm, settling in her chest and screaming that he was his, that he belonged to her… that everything would be okay if Gabe was right here with her, forever. It just made sense. Gabe made sense. There wasn't any other response other than to pull her hand back, grab onto his shoulders, and pull him to her.

Something else took control of her body, and she went with it. Gabe's hands were everywhere, brushing across her stomach, traveling up her thighs, and setting her skin ablaze. His teeth pulled at her bottom lip, gently coaxing her, and she complied, opening her lips and deepening the kiss.

He was growling deep in his chest, and she couldn't help running her hands across the muscles on his back and coming across his chest, feeling his muscles tense, relax, and then tense again. He pulled back suddenly, eyes flashing between his and his beast, but for once, Charlotte couldn't find it in her to be afraid.

"What was that?" he asked, panting as though he had run a marathon.

Charlotte was not in a much better shape. She shook her head with her eyes wide. "I thought you were lying," she muttered breathlessly.

Gabe grinned broadly, leaning his head in to run his nose up the curve of her neck, causing a shiver to course through her skin. "I told you, I can't lie to you." He kissed her gently right where her shoulders and neck connected.

"Gabe can you—" She let out a huff of breath, closing her eyes tight to try to gain control of herself. "Can you step back for a second?"

She thought he wouldn't at first, that he would hold her on his porch for the rest of the day, and Charlotte would not even mind it, but then he took in a deep breath, capturing her scent deep in his lungs, and released her quickly. He took two big steps back, and she watched him in fascination as he regained control of the beast within him.

"Sorry." She breathed out quietly, unable to tear her eyes from him. "I just... I just need a second."

Gabe nodded stiffly while clenching and unclenching his fists. "It's okay." He swallowed, and when met Charlotte's eyes, he was in complete control again. "That was... intense."

Charlotte scratched the back of her neck and blushed wildly. "I thought maybe if it were true I would just see the claim and that'd be it. I didn't think that, you know... I would attack you."

Gabe grinned broadly, making his face about seventeen times more attractive. She fought herself to not jump on him for the second time, and his grin widened like he knew the battle she was fighting. "I certainly didn't mind."

Charlotte let out a groan and dropped down so she was sitting on one of the porch steps, head in her hands. "This is a complete mess," she mumbled. "This is a complete and utter mess."

Not saying a word, Gabe quietly sat beside her and pulled her into his side while Charlotte desperately tried finding something to still hate Gabe about. Of course, there was the whole kidnapping thing. That was ridiculous although he did save her life in the process.

What about the whole cursing his town thing? Although that turned out to be her grandma's fault, it was as much as his grandfather's. How about the fact that her family thought she was dead, that beasts were still roaming her streets and stealing humans, and that apparently, her grandmother was some sort of another species, which meant Charlotte wasn't exactly human either.

God, her head was definitely hurting her now, but with Gabe pulling her close to his side, it was easy to ignore her racing thoughts for just a second and think of the way his soul felt like it was made just for her and how she had lost everything unimportant the moment she felt it.

Chapter 12

As king of the beasts, there were few things that made Gabe chaotic. Several things made him nervous. Other things worried him, too, but there was little to nothing that could make all of his thoughts jumble up and drown.

Charlotte happened to be responsible for about ninety percent of those little to no things.

When he got word that the perimeter was breached by the rogues, his first thought had been of Charlotte. He had left her at his house to do his walk through town. It was important to not lose contact with his pack, no matter how much he wanted to lock him and Charlotte away and create a world just for the two of them.

Charlotte, still being on crutches despite being nearly healed, of course, stayed back. She was still struggling with most of the truths Gabe had shown her, and as such, he was giving her space. Not that he wanted to at all.

When his warriors told him of the breached south perimeter, one of the few weak points in their boundary, Gabe had barked out an order to track the rogues down before taking off to his house. His beast clawed at the surface, begging to be let free, but he couldn't allow it until he knew he had to. If Charlotte saw him as a beast, it could set them back.

About a street away from his house, though, her scream cut straight to his long buried soul and threatened to tear him in half. His beast took control within a blink of an eye, and Gabe didn't fight it. His beast was stronger and quicker. Charlotte needed stronger and quicker if her scream told him anything.

There were four wolves, and he could smell them instantly. A rogue had a rot to their smell, a slowly diminishing scent. Without an official pack link, they slowly grow mad. Beasts were naturally a pack animal. They thrived off the Alpha's leadership and the pack mate's support. Without it, even if they traveled in small groups, they slowly died.

His Charlotte was on the front lawn, limping over the green grass with sweat lining her brow. He was three houses down, and Gabe could see every little detail about her. Her head snapped up at the sound of his approach, and she froze, another scream bubbling in the back of her throat before she stopped.

"Gabe?" she asked, more to herself than to him. "*Gabe*! Gabe they got in the house—"

Just on cue, two of them came barreling out the front door, snarling after his Charlotte. He couldn't remember running so fast in his entire life. In the space of a few seconds, he was there, knocking into one of the wolves as it launched for his mate.

His pack mates would arrive soon. They would figure out the commotion, eventually. He just hoped it would be sooner rather than later as the remaining two wolves came from around the side of the house. His neighbors had left already, receiving the warning of the rogues and moving towards the center of the town. If Gabe had been with Charlotte, he would have taken her to safety too.

Charlotte ran again, and Gabe thanked her silently. If she stayed close, she would get caught in the crossfire. He needed her to be safe to think rationally. Gabe killed the first wolf quickly. There wasn't much of a challenge, but then again, he shouldn't be Alpha if a mere rogue presented a challenge. The other three circled him, snarling, and Gabe baited them, just buying his time.

The wolf on his left launched at him, distracting him, while the one to his right also came at him. He felt canines sink into his flank, the third wolf making an appearance, while the other two tried to bring him down. "Gabe!" Charlotte cried, sharpening his senses better than they had ever been. He felt the canines leave his flank, heard the wolf moving away, and a panic settled into his chest.

He threw the wolf off from his right side and caught the other wolf in the side with his claws, quickly killing him a second later. He nearly stumbled over himself when Charlotte cried out once more.

The wolf was on top of her, snarling, his teeth clamped down on her cast. Charlotte gasped, hitting the wolf's side and trying to keep the teeth away from tender flesh. Gabe took a running step and fell limp from the wound on his back leg. Snarling at his own deficiency, he forced his limbs to move.

When the rogue released the cast and reared back, giving himself enough force to come down on Charlotte, Gabe's world seemed to stop.

There was a pair of rotting teeth glinting in the sunlight, a shoulder it bit into, and the gurgled scream of his mate. Her pain became his until Gabe was snarling from the intensity of it. What he didn't expect was for the other living wolf to barrel into the rogue attacking Charlotte. The newest rogue snarled at the other, but Gabe had no time to ponder over it. Charlotte was choking on her own blood, and they were still alive.

When Gabe got close enough, they hardly cast him a glance before running off. They disappeared behind his house, and he heard them enter the woods. Knowing they were far away enough, Gabe shifted, falling limp with the pain in his thigh by Charlotte's side.

The wolf had nicked her jugular, and Charlotte's hands were grasping her throat to try to stop the bleeding. Her wide eyes found Gabe's as he fell by her side. His hands went to her shoulder and neck, pressing down while he called out for help. She couldn't breathe. His Charlotte was choking, dying...

Oh, god. Oh *god*...

Without thinking, Gabe kneeled down. "Bite me," he said, leaning close to her mouth. She gargled some sort of protest, but Gabe only snarled while pressing his wrist against her mouth. "Bite me! Damn it, Charlotte, you won't die again! Bite me!"

He felt her jaw working and saw her face paling as the blood flowed out from between his fingers. He could hear his pack members coming now, but they would be too late if Charlotte didn't hurry the hell up.

Her small incisors tore his skin and sunk deep into his flesh. She gagged, maybe from her own blood or maybe from Gabe's, but she had bit him. He gritted his teeth and closed his eyes as he felt pieces of his soul falling into place, feeling the beast within him sated unconditionally with her sign of acceptance for their bond. His powers and his strength flowed into her, and as her consciousness faded, her skin began to stitch itself back together.

Gabe sat in the living room of the healer's house. His Charlotte had been there more than his own house, and that unsettled him greatly. "They weren't trying to kill her," he said to his second in command. Odin heaved a sigh.

"The dog went for her jugular." He spat in disgust. Charlotte was as much Odin's queen as Gabe was his king. Any attack against her was against the entire pack, and it unsettled Odin as much as it upset Gabe. "That's a kill shot."

"I think he lost control," Gabe muttered. He rubbed his hand down his jaw. He was exhausted, and the bite on his wrist has healed but scarred by a beautiful, pale indent. "He's a rogue, they have little control, to begin with. The other one stopped him, pushed him off when he saw that he was killing Charlotte."

Odin was silent, and they sat together quietly. The sound of footsteps on the stairs had Gabe looking up as the healer emerged. "Well?" Gabe asked, standing upon her entrance.

"Sit, King, you'll wear yourself out," the old woman commanded. Gabe was helpless to do so. "You're lucky you gained enough of her trust for her to bite you. She would have died otherwise."

"I know that." Gabe snapped, unable to help himself. "I'm—I'm sorry. I just need to know if she'll survive."

"Because the bite was voluntary, it was seen as acceptance of the bond from your beasts' point of view. Without a complete bond, she won't be as powerful as you, but it was enough to stop the bleeding. She'll have a nasty scar, and she'll be sore, but she'll be alright."

Gabe heaved a sigh, feeling his muscles relax for the first time in several hours. He subconsciously rubbed the mark on his wrist, staring into the fire across from him. "She's an elder's descendant," he announced to the healer. The old woman lifted an eyebrow, her sign of complete surprise. "I don't think her mother shows signs of it, but Charlotte certainly does. They were training her to take a spot on the council."

"Does she know this?" Odin asked, just as surprised as the healer.

Gabe shook his head. "She thinks they were just teaching her runes for the hell of it. Have you ever heard of a beast mating with an elder's descendent?" he asked.

Both Odin and the healer shook their heads. "I don't think it's ever happened before," Odin admitted. "I don't think it was ever supposed to happen."

He rubbed his mark once more. "Do you think it'll affect the mating?"

The healer was silent, pondering the question. "It may. She has as much power to offer as you do. Usually, it's one sided. The beast gives the power, and the human accepts it. I don't know what'll happen when she gets your full power. As it is, she'll be much more than she was from just biting you."

Gabe rubbed his temples, feeling an urge to go up to Charlotte and sit by her side. He was standing to do just that when he heard her soft voice traveling down the stairs, small from just waking. "Gabe?"

He couldn't help going to her and sitting beside her on the bed for the following night and half the following day while she healed, hand held in his, a rogue attack fresh on his mind.

Chapter 13

While Gabe slept in the chair beside her, Charlotte inspected the bite on his wrist. Only being conscious enough to beg inchoherently for Gabe to stay by her side—a fact she was much embarrassed by now that she was lucid—she didn't have much to remember other than the ache and fire coursing through her veins.

Now, it was all very much real and very much vivid… the wolves and the way they seemed to come from nowhere, how Charlotte was so certain of her death until Gabe showed up, and the wolves attacking him, too. The thought of him dying seemed so much more absurd and horrific than her own death.

Teeth clamping down on her shoulder, Gabe hollering at her, and instinct forcing her teeth into his wrist. Even now, her soul was turning and twisting, bending with the new power he had given her. Being so attuned with energy, Charlotte was nearly overwhelmed with the shift within her. Charlotte had been privy to certain runes because of the state of her soul, but none of those runes ever affected her the way Gabe was now. She had never felt so... connected.

With the pads of her finger, she traced the pale marks her teeth had left in his skin. She should feel sick about it, shouldn't she? She had bitten Gabe, scarred him for crying out loud, yet she doesn't feel guilty. It seemed very fitting to have him walking around, sporting that sort of mark on his skin like he was telling everyone he was taken, and Charlotte liked that idea.

"You should be sleeping," a deep voice mumbled, thick with sleep. Charlotte's eyes flickered up to piercing blue ones, and she blushed furiously and pulled her hand back from his before sitting more upright in the bed.

"I've been sleeping for an entire day," Charlotte countered. "And besides, I feel fine."

Waking more now, Gabe shifted in his seat, trying to regain feeling in his long legs. Just the beginnings of the morning rays were shining through the clouds in the sky, casting orange hues through the healer's bedroom. "Fine?" he questioned.

Swallowing thickly, Charlotte nodded, feeling an ache in her neck as she did so. "Great, actually." Blushing more, she couldn't help letting her eyes wander to the mark on his wrist. "I-I... Well, thank you."

Gabe grabbed onto her hands and pulled her close so her legs swung off the edge of the bed and their knees were touching. His face was close to hers when her eyes flickered up to his, and her breath caught in her throat. She could feel him, everything about him, coursing through her body. Looking into his eyes now meant looking into his very being. Every hidden message Charlotte had never been able to decipher was explicitly written there, and it stole her breath.

"I would give my own life first before I see yours get taken," he solemnly swore. A free hand came up, brushed over her cheek, and elicited a tremor through her body. His eyes that saw everything did not miss it, and a small grin tugged at the corner of his lips. "Are you not going to bombard me with questions?"

Was she? She supposed she should. She should ask why biting him gave her this power, why those wolves were there in the first place, why she almost died, and if she would be attacked again anytime soon.

For once, though, her questions seemed unimportant. Well, besides one.

"My cast?" she asked, motioning to her pale, bare arm, "and my brace?"

Gabe grinned, splitting his face into a thing of beauty. "Perfectly healed."

Charlotte grinned back, knowing it had been through him that she now felt this invigorated. Steeling herself quickly, and doing it before she could think better of it, she leaned forward and caught his lips with her own. There was something about him now, something undeniable, something she couldn't ignore. He called to her. His soul was in hers now, melding with her own, and it seemed wrong not to connect with him.

Shocked, Gabe sat still. With his muscles tense and his hand tightening around hers, Charlotte suddenly felt very unsure and very foolish. Did he not want her? She started to pull back, opening her eyes just in time to catch a flash of blue before his hand was in her hair and on her hip, pulling her back to him with a burning hunger.

His touch seemed to ignite everything within her. Where Charlotte had been careful, and hesitant, Gabe was sure and undaunted. He kissed Charlotte like he had been doing it his whole life and Charlotte kissed him back like she had so much to catch up on.

She was on his lap without realizing she had moved, her own hands in that magnificent hair of his, tugging and eliciting a low growl from the back of his throat. She could feel her excitement mingled with his own in her very veins, pumping blood through her body.

His hand kneaded against her hip, drew slow patterns right at the juncture. Charlotte hummed, her thoughts clouding suddenly as his other hand massaged the back of her neck, making every muscle loose and relaxed, melding to his touch.

Charlotte did not stop his massive wandering hand as it brushed up under her loose white shirt, gliding across her abdomen. In fact, she leaned closer, encouraging his touch that made her skin feel like it was on fire. Only when his fingers brushed the underside of her breast did Charlotte pull back, gasping loudly.

Catching him off guard, Gabe did not have the time to catch her as she squealed and fell from his lap, landing harshly on the wooden floor.

Instantly, he reached down for her, only to be stopped by the bell-like sound of her laugh. She looked up at him through that curtain of wild hair, her green eyes alight and blessing Gabe with a smile until he was smiling too, then laughing right along with his precious little mate.

She reached up, and using the bed for support, pulled herself to her feet. Her face was red from the laughing and embarrassment, from the after burn of Gabe's touch, and she tried to hide it by tucking her chin to her chest. "I'm sorry," she admitted.

Gabe smiled slyly, knowing she wasn't sorry, that she quite enjoyed Gabe touching her like that, and he very much did as well. She was accepting their bond with the aid of her bite, and it pleased both the human and the beast to an endless extent.

Gabe reached out and grabbed her hips, pulling her forward and causing her to squeal. She stepped between his parted legs, placing her hands on his shoulders for support while he sat in the small wooden chair. He was so much taller than her, that even though she was standing, she was only a few inches taller than his sitting figure. She met his eyes and lost her train of thought instantly.

"Don't ever apologize for that." He grinned, lifting a hand to run the pad of his thumb over her bottom lip.

After a moment, her grin fell, and she sighed, leaning into the support of his hands. "I think I should ask some questions now," she said.

Laughing, Gabe stood up and grabbed her hand to lead her from the room. "I was wondering when you'd ask."

They sat on a shore of a lake Charlotte hadn't known existed until Gabe showed her. With trees at their back and crystal, flat water to their front, Gabe had never seen his Charlotte so relaxed.

He leaned back on his hands and watched her fidget, inconspicuously trying to move closer to him on the rocks they lounged on. With the sun doing a steady climb in the sky now, the heat was coming to the air right along with it.

"You don't have to hide it, you know," Gabe said with a sly grin.

Charlotte whipped her head around, almost catching Gabe in the face with her hair. "What?" she asked innocently.

"You can touch me and be near me. I'll never deny you."

She blushed again, something rare for Charlotte, but Gabe was coming to love it. She swallowed, and surprised him by moving in close enough so their legs, spread out in front of them, touched. She was usually so stubborn, he figured she would stand, huff, and then walk half a mile away just to spite him.

"I don't know why I can't touch you," she admitted quietly.

Still sitting somewhat in front of him, Gabe could smile without her seeing. It was a gentle smile, his eyes like a caress as they moved over her fiery hair, across her shoulders, to the hand just behind her. He grabbed onto it and held it within his much larger one. "It's your body needing to complete the bond."

Gabe spent most of the morning discussing what her bite meant. How it tied their souls together, how it was a sign for his inner beast that she accepted him and allowed his power, his very soul, to pour into hers.

Interested yet again, Charlotte held onto his hand while she angled her body more to look at him. "How?"

"How do you complete your part of the bond?" she nodded. "You need to open your soul to me."

Upon the instant drain of color from her face, Gabe sat up straight and pulled her close. "You can't just bite me back?" she asked in a small voice that had the beast in him waking up, wondering what was causing Charlotte to cower suddenly.

"No—I mean, if you were human, yes. But you're not, and for interspecies mating to work, each half must be completed by that species code. My code was biting. That's why you bit me. The code of your people is to bare your soul, to which I will bind myself." When she was silent once more, his chest tightened. "What? What's wrong?"

Shaking her head as she lowered her eyes, she could feel every one of her muscles tense under his touch. "It's nothing." She lied lamely.

"Charlotte, what's wrong?" He persisted, his voice harder. She wasn't going to start hiding from him now, was she?

Sighing, she lifted her eyes back up to his. "I don't know if I can ever complete my side of the bond." She admitted in barely a whisper.

Gabe cocked his head to the side like he couldn't quite understand what she was saying. "What do you mean?"

She licked her dry lips. "M-my soul, my granddad he— Jeez, Gabe, I'm sorry." She let out a huff of air, wincing. "I didn't know what completing the bond meant. I didn't know things like this existed. I thought I was going to escape you and go back home and you'd be like a bad dream. I didn't have a reason to tell you before."

His hands moved to her shoulders, an unease settling in Gabe's gut. "Tell me what, Charlotte?"

She winced again like she was saying the words in her head again and again and it was beating her down each time. Her shaking fingers reached for the hem of her shirt, and in a fluid movement, displacing Gabe's hands from her shoulders, she took the shirt off. Shocked at the sudden movement, Gabe wondered idly what the hell she was doing.

She placed a hand at the top of her left breast, right over her heart. If it weren't for the tense circumstances, Gabe would have admired the milky skin exposed to him and the swell of her breasts encased in black lace. "Charlotte—"

Her hand slipped from the skin, revealing a jagged scar atop her creamy skin. "My soul's locked, Gabe," she said quietly. Lifting one of his hands, Gabe traced the small scar with his finger. Charlotte's hand came up over his hand, flattening his palm over her heart. "It was the only way to save me. Only the elders can open it."

Her words drifted over him like his mind refused to process them. His beast roared in his ears, demanding some justice for this. The scar beneath his palm seemed to burn him, an unmistakable stab wound from a lethal knife. The elders, her grandmother, had done the only thing they could to keep Charlotte alive with such a grave wound. They locked her soul to the body, refusing to give it transport to the afterlife. How painful had that been for his Charlotte? How much energy had that required? He had heard stories of that sort of power but never saw proof. Not until now. Not until his Charlotte.

"Who?" Gabe choked out, meeting her eyes. "Who did this?"

"Locked it? My grandma—"

Gabe shook his head. "No, this." He pulled his hand back, tracing her scar once more. "Who did this to you?"

Charlotte winced like it still hurt her, and Gabe pulled away instantly. She ran a hand through her knotted hair and sighed. "My granddad tried to kill me when I was nine years old. Ran a steak knife into my chest. Gabe, I... God, I shouldn't have bit you. I can feel everything from you, and I never meant—Gabe, please, I'm so sorry. I don't know how to complete the bond. I can't. If my soul is unlocked, I'm going to die."

Gabe shut his eyes tight, already feeling the agony of being unbound to her. It was fine now. He just needed to be closer to her. Later, though... later they would go mad.

He opened his eyes to see tears in hers, and he cupped her face in his too large hands and brought her closer to place gentle lips atop hers. "We'll figure this out." He swore.

Gabe could only hope.

Chapter 14

Gabe watched her from a distance, debating with himself quietly. She was running her hands through a soft fabric Sabrina had woven and was selling in the market. She was too far for him to make out her laugh, but he had it memorized and could imagine it clearly.

What monster could ever try to kill anything as perfect as her?

His chest tightened, beast snarling, at the thought of her gone... dead. He never would have met her, never had a mate, never been complete, and now, he still may very well not be. If they couldn't figure out how to keep her alive, the two of them would go mad.

"What's got you silent and brooding?" the voice of his old friend asked. Odin walked up the street and stood next to Gabe, who leaned against the side of a house, ankles crossed and blue eyes hard.

He shook his head and remained silent.

He had given Charlotte money to spend, and as queen, people had been offering her free things the entire afternoon, but she had not accepted a single item. It was frustrating still not knowing so much about her. How could he possibly know what her favorite color was if she looked at each vibrant cloth with equal admiration? How could he ever discover if she even liked flowers when she passed them with just a small look and a slight smile? She was utterly fascinating, but she gave nothing away. It was like every little thing the world had to offer, she enjoyed.

"You only brood like this when you're about to do something stupid," Odin continued, despite the fact Gabe clearly didn't want to discuss anything. "As your friend and your second in command, I take it as my responsibility to ensure you don't do anything stupid."

Finally, Gabe glanced over at his friend. Charlotte already craved Gabe, and he knew it. Just the slight changes in her behavior, how she stood a step closer to him, and how she 'accidentally' kept brushing his hand gave her away. She wanted him despite her conscious rebelling, and oh, how Gabe wanted Charlotte just as much.

To save her and to save himself, he had no choice but to do something stupid.

"Can you watch her tonight?"

Odin lifted an eyebrow. "You are leaving her? You haven't been away from her side since she got here."

Gabe grunted. He knew that perfectly well. Odin certainly didn't need to point it out. It would be brutally painful to leave her even for a second. He had no choice, though.

Charlotte knew nothing about who he really was, what she could really do.

Gabe needed to go to the people who knew.

"Tell her I went on a patrol or something."

"You don't go on patrol."

"I know, Odin, but thank you for reminding me. Just tell her."

They were quiet, and Gabe felt a thrill in his gut when Charlotte handed over money in exchange for a small bag of sweets. Did his mate have a sweet tooth? He wouldn't have expected it, but it was enough to figure out something about her.

He watched her turn and bend down to a small blonde-haired girl standing beside her and handed the bag over. Charlotte said something completely age inappropriate to the girl if Gabe could read her lips right, but the blonde, Kate he remembered, laughed anyways. She looked up then, still smiling, to catch Gabe's eye.

She gave him a dazzling smile, one that did odd things to his head, making him feel like he could die a happy man knowing she was smiling like that for him.

She began walking through the thick crowd, nodding and greeting people she passed who addressed her. "I won't be gone for longer than an hour," Gabe said suddenly.

"You're going on the run?" Odin asked although it was more like a statement than a question. "If she finds out, she'll be crushed. She'll think you're finding someone el—"

"So she won't find out," Gabe hissed. His consciousness was already at war enough over this entire ordeal, couldn't Odin see that? Gabe was out of options.

Charlotte was close now, almost within hearing range. "Look, something's gone wrong with our mating. It's half complete and can't be finished. I need to find a solution, and she cannot know where I'm going to find that solution. Alright?"

Solemn faced and slightly mortified, Odin nodded. The thought of a half-finished mating was… appalling to any beast or man.

"She'll want to go if she knows where you're going."

"Which is why she can't know." Gabe snarled, his beast coming to the front. He had asked Odin as a friend to watch Charlotte, but he was very near to demanding it as his king. "I do not trust those people, or what they were raising her to become. I will not put her in harm's way."

Charlotte broke through the crowd then, moving to stand in front of Gabe. "Do you think I can swim in that lake we visited the other day?" she asked Gabe, her voice light, airy, and capable of sending small, tiny shivers down Gabe's spine.

Only seconds later, as empathetic as she was, she picked up on the tension between the two and frowned, mouth opening in her ever curious way to ask a question when Gabe cut her off.

"We can go now if you'd like."

Still frowning, she nodded. "Sure. Are you alright?"

He offered her a smile, but she already had her side of the mating bond. She could feel Gabe, feel his very soul. She knew him now, and as such, knew every secret he tried and failed to hide from her.

She could also tell, then, what things she should ask about and what things she should not.

"I was thinking I—or you, rather… could buy some of the sandwiches in the market, and we could just eat down there. Unless you need to be here for work or something. I'm still not entirely sure how you guys manage to sustain a semi-modern society out here in the middle of nowhere."

Gabe cracked another smile, this one more genuine. "We have our ways."

He pushed himself from the edge of the wall and grabbed her hand, and when she didn't pull away, he was mortified at the thought of never having moments like this again.

"Gabe?" Charlotte asked, breathing into his neck.

His hand tightened on her hips, holding her in place. The rocks were warm against his naked back, and the sun was beating down on them. Charlotte, still in her wet clothes, lay atop Gabe. He couldn't remember how they had gotten into this position, nothing sexual had even occurred, yet he could swear he has never been more comfortable.

"Yes?" he asked, running his fingers through the wet knots of her wild hair.

She was silent and seemed to decide not to ask her question. Instead, she sat up. With the sun shining down on her and her pale skin dripping water droplets, she looked like a goddess.

She picked up his wrist, the one she had bitten, and brought it close to trail her hand over it. Jolts shot up his arm and pooled in his chest, making him ache to complete the bond, making him want to turn them over and ravish his beautiful mate until the only thing she knew was his name and the way he made her feel.

"I knew I was different," she mumbled, not looking up to meet his intense stare. "None of the other kids could do what I do. They knew what runes to write if they needed and they had enough power to protect their doorstep, but no one could do what I could do. Grandma said she was training me."

"They wanted you to join the council I bet," Gabe mumbled, finding it hard to focus when she touched her bite mark like that when she was sitting atop him... when her clothes stuck to her like a second skin from her swim.

She shook her head, a strand of fiery red hair falling in front of her eyes. She released his hand to brush it behind her ear, and Gabe was able to find some semblance of thought. "For as long as I can remember, I was trained with the runes, with strengthening my own power and using the energy I had within me to the utmost of my control. They never taught me a single thing about the council, though. Other members were taught from birth to know the rules and law, but they never said a word about it to me."

Gabe's eyebrows came down in thought. "What do you think were they training you for?"

She shrugged and leaned forward to press her palms against his bare chest. He shivered under her touch, and a coy smile graced her face. For a blistering moment, Gabe was blown away by this side of Charlotte, the side of her not buried six feet deep under sarcasm and denial and seventeen different ways to insult someone. "I don't know," she mumbled, but her eyes were glazing over now, distracted.

God, it must be hell for her, Gabe figured, feeling her own want and then feeling Gabe's want as well. Her need to complete the bond was powerful and soon would be painful. Gabe's beast was sated enough having her close, but Charlotte's soul would never be at peace until Gabe truly belonged to her.

"Lately, I can't think that well around you," she admitted quietly, watching her hands as they moved across his skin. "I know it's got to do with this bite thing. I know we talked about this happening, but it's like it's changed my entire perspective on everything. It's terrifying, actually."

Gabe reached up and grabbed her hands, stilling her movements above him. "How do you mean?" he questioned gently.

"I don't want to go home." She shrugged. "I miss my family terribly. I'd love to see them more than anything, but I can't seem to find it in me to want to leave your side. I don't even know half the people living in this never ending town, yet I feel as though it'd be betraying them by leaving."

Gabe's chest tightened. "You're their queen now." He explained. "Your instinct has changed and adapted. You're going to start feeling like a leader more and more."

"And you?" she questioned. "Is *this* going to get worse?"

Gabe knew she was talking about the need, the urge to touch, to kiss, and to caress. It has been nearly a week since she had bitten him, and it had escalated almost exponentially.

Gabe nodded, unable to lie to her. "Until I figure it out."

She smiled wryly. "You sound so confident."

He suddenly pulled her hands out, making her eyes widen in surprise as she crashed forward, bumping her forehead against his. She stared, shocked, down at him, just centimeters away, their lips brushing each other's gently. This, here, was what Gabe always thought of in a mate.. small, tiny moments like this where everything was okay, Charlotte wasn't scared of him, and they had no other worries. He was certain that when she gains some sort of clarity, she would be back to screaming at him and ignoring his every word, but he took comfort at this moment.

"I refuse to let anything happen to you, ever," he said solemnly. "I will defy fate if I have to."

This time, her smile was much sadder. "Alright then." She closed the distance, pressing her lips against his. "I think I'd like to see you try."

The beasts roamed the street on silent paws, traveling the same roads and following the same paths. Like before, like every other time, the king of beasts stood back, standing in the trees in his human form.

At his elevation, he could see the tiny town spread out before him nestled in a valley. His Charlotte loved it here, loved the small houses and the cute shops, loved the seclusion and the forced solitary.

With eyes more beastly than man, he scanned the streets like he used to. A deep, aching pull was drawing him back to his own home where he knew Charlotte was waiting for him.

But luckily, the beast within the man was as adamant about finding some form of connection with their mate. Both man and beast were willing to try anything. Going back now meant failing her, the one person who could ever help heal his demons and could help placate the storm inside of him.

At the howl of one of his pack mates, victorious and loud, and the shrill cry of a girl as she discovered a wolf in her bedroom, the king of beasts transformed to four legs and took off into the streets, the elder's scent in the air.

Chapter 15

Her red hair caught the moonlight, making it look like burning embers. With eyes closed, Charlotte and her naturally pale skin looked like a statue sitting atop a roof, knees pulled up to her chest and face tilted towards the stars.

She was starting to get concerned with her odd obsession with roofs. Gabe would surely throw a fit if he saw her up there.

But that's why she was up there, wasn't it? Because Gabe was gone.

And unfortunately, the distance did odd things to Charlotte's head. It allowed her to think rationally, or maybe not so rationally. All she knew was that she had gotten a headache the moment Gabe left, and she was two seconds away from ripping her own hair out.

Almost self-consciously, without her knowing, she traced that old, ugly scar on her chest. She could feel her heart thumping from under her shirt. She wondered how odd it would feel if she really could connect with Gabe as he described. Even now she felt... incomplete.

"Charlotte, are you coming in soon?" Odin called from the front lawn, neck craned back to stare up at the girl on the roof.

"In a minute," she called back quietly, knowing he could hear.

He paused like he was about to argue before sighing and stepping back into Gabe's house.

Charlotte was having a mental struggle, an odd argument with herself that she couldn't seem to win. It was easy being mad at Gabe when he had dragged her from her family. He had been nothing but the king of beasts to her.

But now he was Gabe, her mate. Now he was Gabe, whose soul flowed into hers, made her half complete, made her feel everything about him, every perfection that outweighed every flaw. He was everything now, and it seemed wrong to be angry at him for any reason.

Yet she was.

Gabe had left to go to her home without her. She wasn't concerned that he had gone on the run, no matter how Odin tried to hide it. Where else would he be in the middle of the night? Charlotte wasn't an idiot. It didn't take her long to figure that one out.

What she was concerned about, however, was that he was hunting down answers in her hometown without her when he knew that the only thing she really wanted was to see her family again.

She thought she wasn't a captive anymore, but with Gabe dictating where she went and Odin watching her like a guard, she felt like a prisoner all over again.

She understood Gabe's concerns. Sort of. The elders had been grooming Charlotte for something, and it could only be trouble. She just…

God, she didn't even know. Her head was being pulled in a hundred different directions, and she could only feel a deep ache in her chest, right under her scar, where her soul yearned to open up to Gabe.

She dreamed of her granddad sometimes. Dreamed of blue-green eyes, the color of a tropical ocean, staring down at her and a knife in her chest. She dreamed of crimson, of blood staining the linoleum and of his fingers drawing runes in the tiles and crying.

She dreamed of her soul as a separate thing, a separate entity of its own being pulled from her body and twisted, warped, and forced from its home.

Charlotte dreamed a lot of that night, but nothing more than the way he had come up to her, had wrapped his arms around her and told her that granddad loves her, his Charlotte, his little girl, and that someday she would understand.

There was no sensation in dreaming, but Charlotte woke up gasping most nights feeling that odd pressure in her chest, the sharp pain, the grunt as the knife was forced through bone and muscle and tissue all over again and fighting off an imaginary man who had been her hero.

Shivering slightly although there was no breeze, Charlotte blinked her eyes and gazed at the forest in front of her.

Gabe was somewhere out there, trying to find answers. He had been searching for Charlotte for years, and all she could give him was a bite to the wrist and a promise to never be able to complete the other half of him. She brought him up, just so she could slowly, block by block, tear him right back down.

Unfortunately, though, Charlotte didn't see much of the forest, too caught up in her own thoughts and by the stars in the sky. Maybe she could have seen the shadows otherwise, moving on their own in the darkness, the eyes blinking up at her, the snarl of rotten teeth and fur matted with blood red runes.

The beasts lurked around every street bend, claws slicing across the pavement and the very air stilling as if to not draw attention to itself. They moved like they were shadows, silent, deadly, and dark.

The moon itself fell behind a cloud, and if you were lucky enough, you had found sleep hours before and were dreaming peacefully. If you were Samantha Mires, then you were on your way back to the beasts home, unconscious in the arms of a running man who looked down at her as though he were carrying gold.

If you were Sydney, then you had landed a solid punch to a naked man's family jewels but hadn't gotten more than three steps before a hand put just the right amount of pressure on the back of your neck. You fell limp, supported by a set of broad arms that didn't dare hold you too tight for fear of breaking something so precious, so unbelievably perfect.

And if you were powerful enough to feel it, feel the beasts lurking in the shadows, then you were deep, very deep, in the very same shadows where they wouldn't even think to look.

In his eternal cage, in the darkness he was swarmed and drowned in, tropical ocean eyes saw into those shadows, watching the king of beasts prowl through the very same streets the king's mate had called home, and waited patiently, just as quietly, for the right time.

Because, as it turned out, his whole life, he had had nothing but time until now when it really mattered. Now, while the king sought after what he knew nothing about, his very mate was dreaming atop a roof with a dozen rabid beasts waiting to bring her home.

Jeremiah Strite, sitting in his dark, dark cage, could wait no longer.

It was time to finish what he had started.

Chapter 16

That was close. That was close. That was close.

Charlotte couldn't seem to shake the thought as she limped into the center of town with five wolves surrounding her, snarling to the pavement like even the road was an enemy. In the distance, she could see the group of women and unshifted children going to the shelter. In the background, she could still hear the snarling.

That was close.

She was no beast, had no beastly traits, but she swore that she could smell her own blood in the night.

There was a piercing howl, shot up to the clouds briefly obscuring the moon, that was cut off with a vicious growl and a sharper yelp. Charlotte winced and felt her insides turn at the thought of one of them being her own. There was no thought towards the fact she considered these people hers now like she really was a queen. Just the fear that someone was dead.

A man, clothed with only a pair of shorts, darted out into the streets. She recognized him as one of Gabe's warriors, a man built like a soldier with broad shoulders and chin lifted high.

"Queen, you'll be in the back of the shelter with no less than three guards at your s—"

"The others?" she cut him off, wincing as her ankle turned on a rock, her bleeding calf screaming in protest. A wolf stepped to her side, offering support. Her fingers dug into his fur that was softer than she had expected, and she mumbled a quiet thanks.

"The other women and children will be guarded as well. Everyone in the shelter is guarded."

"But me more than others?"

There was a pause, then a nod of the head. "You are our queen."

"And as your queen, then, I demand you to put those three men as normal perimeter guards of the shelter. If we get attacked, someone else shouldn't die in my place just because I have a title."

Her lip curled up, disgusted at the thought, and even when the man—Sam, she remembered now—opened his mouth to protest, she cut him off. "Listen, I know Gabe would probably have your head otherwise, but he's not here, is he? He's off doing something I'll yell at him for later if we all get out of this. I think I have a pretty good idea of the authority chain in this place, and that same chain of command puts me in charge since he's gone. I don't want to go about throwing orders, but I will if I have to."

Another pause, and even the wolves surrounding her slowed down in protest. "Alright." Sam conceded, bowing his head. "As you wish."

She nodded then swallowed. "How bad is it?"

"We've got about two dozen rogues," he said, voice cutting to something different, something more usual for a man like him... direct, factual, and comfortable. "They breached our north boundary, as you very well know."

Yes, she did know. Her calf seared to remind her how they had gotten into the living room before Odin stopped them, just long enough for the reinforcements, she hadn't known were so close, to arrive.

"How many—I mean, how many of our own are injured?"

"Three injured, ma'am," he responded quickly, "one dead."

She winced but held her head higher. She didn't know much about this place, but she did know that they were a strong, incredibly durable community. That one man would be mourned like a son by all, but they would fight three times as hard because of his loss.

"How'd they get in without detection? I thought you guys had patrols." After all, that was the bullshit lie Gabe had told her he was doing tonight instead of running off to her old town without her.

To this, Sam had no quick answer, and that seemed to frustrate him. His closely cropped blond hair shifted a bit in the slight breeze, and his thick eyebrows pulled down in irritation.

"We're not sure. They seem to have drawings on their sides in pigs blood from the smell of it, but we've never seen—"

Charlotte froze, hand lashing out to grab onto Sam's arm, pulling him to a stop. The five wolves tensed and turned, looking for a threat and growling with their lips pulled back, but Charlotte could hardly care. Her heart was in her throat, and she felt like she needed to throw up. Earlier, she hadn't noticed anything in the dark other than fur, teeth, and claws. She hadn't seen any runes then.

"What drawings?" she asked, her voice not sounding like her own.

Sam raised an eyebrow, glancing at the nails digging into his bicep. "A bunch of swirls, ma'am. They don't look like anything."

"But they're all the same? The symbol? On every wolf, it's the same symbol?"

Sam nodded slowly, visibly concerned with his own head lifting and searching around them warily, as Charlotte's dread infected the air. "You need to draw it for me. Draw it for me in the dirt, now."

"Ma'am—"

"Now!"

There was no more hesitation, just a quick detour to the side of the road where Sam knelt on one knee and drew into the soft dirt with the pads of his fingers. Charlotte watched with intense green eyes that were so bright in the night that even the beasts had trouble looking. She watched each curve, each swirl, each interconnecting loop being formed. It was like she was back in her lessons, like her grandma was standing beside her, teaching her, testing her.

Her dread was replaced by cold calculation, her mind switching to that ever present, ever tactful logical side.

When Sam was done, he stood and brushed his hands on his shorts then looked at Charlotte. "You know it?"

She nodded her head, thinking so fast, she could hardly grab on to any of her thoughts.

An elder had drawn that, was her first thought. There was no one with enough power, other than the elders, to create a rune of that magnitude.

She couldn't think of the who right now, or the how, or the why.

Right now, she needed to think of a counter strike.

"How fast are they closing in?" Charlotte asked.

Sam's face turned grim, lines hardening across his jaw. "Half our warriors are out on the run, ma'am. We've never had the rogues team up like this before. They're closing in fast."

"Can they hold them five houses back from the west end of town for another twenty minutes?"

There was a pause, a nod.

"Then do it. Send these guys out too. I'd like one to stay with me if that's alright since the only thing I've got is a set of nails that need clipping, but I don't need five."

"What are you thinking, ma'am?" Sam asked, ever the soldier. "Eventually, we'll fall back in further, keeping them five houses out on all sides is only surrounding ourselves."

"That's fine, it won't matter. What I do need is for every wolf on our side, within fifty feet, to be within that perimeter on my signal, got it?"

She didn't give him time to respond. She just started limping in the other direction, calculating distances, runes, and times in her head like she was a calculator. The beasts paused, watching her back for a moment, before swiftly doing as their queen demanded while she silently cursed Gabe for leaving and prayed even quieter for him to be alright.

Barbara Strite was waiting for him on her front porch, sitting in the old wicker rocking chair with a cup of sweet iced tea beside her.

She didn't look like a grandma. In fact, she could rival most thirty-year-old mothers with her strawberry blonde hair piled in a neat bun atop her head, pink lipstick so sharp and proud, and green eyes vibrant and full of endless life. There wasn't a single wrinkle on her beautiful face, not even one worry line. She sat proud and tall in her chair as Gabe approached and even motioned to a pair of shorts resting on the matching chair beside her.

"I assumed you'd like to have this conversation clothed," she announced to the beast before her, unfazed by those intense, iridescent blue eyes. The beast stayed still, calculating the woman before him, before padding up the porch steps and grabbing the shorts with his irreducibly daunting teeth.

He disappeared into the shadows, only to return a moment later in his human, sculpted glory, still moving in that careful way as though he expected the three hundred-something-year-old woman to draw a knife and shank him in the side.

Barbara motioned to the now empty chair, but Gabe didn't move from his spot by the porch railing. "If you insist on standing, I have no problem," she said, sighing deeply. She grabbed her tea and took a gentle sip. "Although I can assure you that you're in no danger."

Gabe didn't move.

"This is about my granddaughter, yes?" No answer. "Her soul?"

To that, Gabe tensed ever so slightly, but she saw and offered a gentle smile. "I've seen the scar," Gabe said, his first words stated aloud. His voice was stiff and rough, the beast still tumbling right under his skin.

Barbara frowned, revealing the first wrinkles Gabe had seen on her face. "Yes, what a terrible day that was," she muttered, more to herself than to him. "Jeremiah surprised us all, I'm afraid."

"Tell me how to fix it," Gabe demanded. "Tell me how to unlock her soul without killing her."

Another sad smile was offered, to which Gabe wanted to strangle the old woman. He didn't want sympathy. He wanted solutions. "That's the point, my dear. Locking her soul was the only way to keep her alive. There's no way for her to live without it in place."

Inside, his beast roared, but on the outside, Gabe didn't move a muscle. "There's another way." It wasn't a fact, just a demand.

"Sit down, please. I insist." When he didn't, she heaved a heavy sigh. "Jeremiah was a sick man. He knew our Charlotte had a very, very powerful soul, one that could rival our own. He wanted to harness it for his own. When we arrived, we were able to pull my husband away from her, but she already had a blade through her heart. Her soul was leaking out onto the kitchen floor right beside her blood. It was... beautiful, her soul. I've never seen anything quite like it. She was dying, Gabriel, like most people do when stabbed in the chest.

"There is no hope of saving a human with such a wound. They have fragile souls that like to slip through the cracks. It'd be like locking gas in a wiffle ball, but Charlotte isn't human, as I believe you've discovered. The only way to really, really save her was to take her soul and lock it within her own body. Now we've locked the gas in a seamless steel cage with no chance of escaping, unless you drill a hole in it like you're insisting you do. The gas will just slip out. You can't grab it. You can't hold onto it, and you can only watch it go."

Gabe snarled and threw his fist against one of the porch beams. "Where is he?"

"Jeremiah? Oh, he's locked away, dear. My husband is in a place where there is no chance of escaping. You have nothing to worry about."

"I'm not worried about his escape," he breathed out through clenched teeth. His beast was snarling, itching to be let out, to go home, to be with his Charlotte whose soul he could never be fully with. And that ached somewhere deep, deep within him.

Barbara sighed once more. "Well, then I'm afraid it's not that easy to kill one of us. We're a tricky species."

"I will find a way!" he roared, shaking the house on its hinges and waking the neighbors. The beasts were still roaming, though, and as such, not a single light turned on and not a single head poked out from behind the curtains to investigate.

"If you were to bring her back, I could look." Barbara offered, standing to her small height as she spoke. "There's not much hope, but I can try."

That was... off. Gabe was a keen and calculating ruler. He knew how to size an enemy up, how to read everything about them with one look, and Barbara was far too eager.

"Why have you not come for her yourself if you knew?"

"It's in our agreement," she said. "I cannot harm your people any more than you can harm mine, and I certainly cannot take a mate."

They were silent for a moment, both agreeing for once.

"This Jeremiah, her grandfather, would he know anything? Someway to reverse what he'd started?"

She was silent, head tilted to the side. "He knows no more than me."

"But it's a possibility."

"Gabriel—"

"Ask him," he demanded, standing to his full height. "You and your kind condemned my mate to this. You owe her. Ask him."

Her eyes hardened to green slates, her jaw clenching. "Fine," she relented, her voice sharp. She disappeared into the house, then returned with a small piece of charcoal. She drew on the railing beside Gabe. It was by far the most complicated rune he had ever seen, looking like four interconnecting ones that Barbara drew so seamlessly. There was no doubt she had been doing it for a long time.

She pressed her hand to it and to Gabe. It seemed like she had only blinked before her hand retracted, a gasp escaping her lips. Several emotions splashed over her face, first surprise, then confusion, then fury. Her eyes blazed a forest green, her teeth grinding.

"He's gone," she said, turning on her heel to disappear into the house once again.

Gabe, confused beyond his wits, took only a moment longer to realize his mate's attempted killer was gone from whatever impenetrable prison they had him in, and Charlotte was by herself.

He leaped from the porch, turning into a beast mid-leap, and howled into the night sky just as the moon broke free

Chapter 17

It looked like a bomb was dropped just outside of his town.

The beast was in full control, in full power. His legs pushed past lifeless rogue bodies, frozen with their beastly eyes open in wonder at whatever had taken place before them.

The beast could smell the power, the energy, lingering in the air like smoke and sticking to everything. The trees were flattened to the ground and ripped from their roots, branching out in a circle and tightening towards a center.

He could see them, a group of twenty or so of his warriors standing on shaken legs. They watched him approach, and as one, they stepped back from the shaking form on the ground, fingers digging into the soil.

A whine passed the beasts lips as he saw a mass of tangled red hair. The wind swept, hiding her face, and she pressed her cheek to the ground and shuddered, trembled, and jolted.

He stopped at her side, breathing in deep. He smelled blood, saw the wound on her calf already half healed, and knew there must be some on her palm too. His Charlotte had to have used a rune. There was no other explanation for the disaster around them. She must have used her own blood once more.

He fell down on his stomach in front of her, and gently, as gently as a beast could manage, touched his nose to the exposed pale skin of her cheek.

Her eyes fluttered, green orbs unfocused on the scattered forest floor, before looking up to the beast kneeling before her. "Gabe?" she asked, voice just hardly above a whisper. He whined, rubbing his nose along the side of her face.

"You're in so much trouble," she said breathlessly and tried to laugh, only to shut her eyes close and grit her teeth. "I mean it."

Beside them, Odin turned back to a man standing on two feet with his head bowed to his two rulers. "They had runes on them, sir," he announced when Charlotte seemed incapable of forming her own words. "It gave them power, an ability to work with one another and evade our borders and warriors. She, she drew some runes on the trees beyond this perimeter. I think it took her more than she told us it would."

Words drifted through his ears, and they couldn't seem to stick to his mind. His Charlotte was shaking like a leaf, desperately trying to gain hold of herself once more.

"I'd very much like you to turn back into a guy with two arms and two legs, please," she faintly mumbled. She opened her eyes and lifted them to his brilliant blue ones. "I won't even complain that you're naked."

She would have complained anyways, but she knew now was not the time for jokes. It was natural to do as she asked, and his human form came to life, quickly grabbing hold of his mate and pulling her into his arms.

"What in the world were you thinking?" he asked, cradling her against his chest while he pressed his lips to her dirt covered temple.

"I was thinking that the king of these people was off running around my old town, and that we were outnumbered, and that an elder is trying to kill me, and I had no choice."

He grimaced at each item she ticked off, feeling his own self-hatred grow by the second. "Well, I can't quite yell at you anymore, can I?"

She hummed in agreement, trying to pull herself closer to him. "Can we go, please? I can feel their souls leaving, and it's quite disturbing."

Like a flash, he was on his feet, carrying her in his arms like a bride. Her arms wound around his neck, hanging on. His bare feet crunched on the flattened sticks and grass that coiled around the turned over roots and tree trunks.

"I'm so sorry I wasn't here."

"I'm almost glad you weren't." She sighed. He glanced down at her, more confused than anything. "You never would have let me attempt what I did back there otherwise."

He passed the first line of standing trees, glanced quickly at the blood drawn into the dark wood, then looked back at her. "What did you do exactly?"

She frowned and ducked her face against him so her fiery hair hid her face. "I did what I needed to do to protect the town. I don't want to talk about it, really."

"Alright," he said, rubbing his hand down her arm. "That's alright."

When they entered the town, the women and children were starting to come out onto the streets, going where they knew the commotion had gone down. They drew to either side of the road at the sight of their king cradling their queen and bowed their heads as he passed.

Behind him, the rest of the beasts on the run returned, diving through the darkened trees and back into town. They had no mates or children yet, but everyone in the town was family despite that.

He avoided the healer, knowing it would do her no good. Despite her weakness now, she was still tapped into Gabe's own energy and would heal faster than ever before if the wound on her leg was of any indication.

The inside of his house was destroyed, and claw marks and the smell of rot covered almost every surface. His couch cushions were torn and gutted, the white fluff making it look like a sea of foam had covered the carpet. He smelled Charlotte's blood in there and knew she had been cut at this point.

"Odin is quite the fighter." She sighed against him.

"I'm so sorry." He closed his eyes and began climbing the stairs, his guilt a terrible thing within.

"Oh, shut up," she mumbled, snuggling closer to him. "What did you find out?"

He kicked his bedroom door open and crossed the room, and as gently and carefully as he could, laid her down. "I'm going to grab a cloth."

He escaped the room quickly, wetting a washcloth in his bathroom as he tried to collect his thoughts. How could he tell her that her grandfather, the man who tried to kill her when she was a child, was out, and was apparently coming for her now if the rogues carrying runes were of any indication?

When she called out to him with her voice so soft, he had no choice but to return. He sat at the edge of the bed and carefully lifted her injured leg, healed besides a faint red line. He ran the cloth up her leg, wiping the dried blood away, focusing so much, he could hardly feel her eyes boring into him.

"Gabe." She grabbed his attention and held it when her green eyes met him. "What happened?"

He dropped the washcloth on the floor beside the bed and moved closer to her. "I met with Barbara."

She raised an eyebrow. "My grandma? What'd she say?"

Almost unconsciously, her hand moved to her chest and covered the scar beneath her white shirt.

He opened his mouth to speak then closed it again. She could feel everything he felt after all. She would be able to feel his torment loud and clear.

There was a flash of something in her eyes before a mask hid it. She shifted on the bed, cleared her throat, then grabbed onto Gabe's hand. "It's alright. We're alright."

He nodded because he didn't have to tell her she was wrong. She already knew.

"There's something else," he forced himself to say.

"It can't get much worse, so let me have it."

Again, she felt how wrong she was, and she raised herself up on the bed, eyebrows coming down in concern. "What is it? What's wrong?"

"Jeremiah escaped. He's gone. I think he... I think he did something to the rogues."

"Granddad?"

His silence was her confirmation, and he watched closely as her coping mechanism kick-started. He could see the quick working of logic behind her eyes, of plans being formed, of anything to ignore the emotional side of things and just focus on the intellectual.

"Okay," she said slowly, eyes flickering over the bed as though looking over a memory. "Okay, alright. We know who did the runes on the rogues now. We know what he's after."

Her nails scratched at the scar, and when it was hard enough to hurt, she jolted from her thoughts, her eyes flying up to Gabe's.

"Charlotte—"

"He read me stories as a kid," she blurted out, her head shaking and her wild frizzy strands of hair clouding her face, "and he'd let me sit on his lap, and when mom made one of her terrible dinners, I could go to their house, and he'd make me a steak. I don't... I don't know why he wants me dead so bad." She swallowed thick, her eyes wide. "I don't know why he doesn't love me anymore."

Gabe pulled her to him carefully, wrapping his arms around her body while she shuddered from exhaustion and despair. "I won't let anything happen to you."

She scoffed in his arms but hung onto him, regardless. "You don't know what the elders are capable of. If he wants me dead, then—"

"Don't." His arms tightened. "Don't say it. Nothing is going to happen to you."

She was silent for a long, long moment, listening to his heart beating beneath his shirt. "Alright," she whispered into the dark room.

They sat around a long oval table, the dark wood worn and carrying the obvious signs of wear and tear. There were twelve of them, the thirteenth chair remaining vacant and a bowl of incense burning in the center.

"Jeremiah is out of containment," Barbara Strite announced to the gathered crowd of elders the moment the last of them sat. A collective murmur rose among the group, and there were disquieted shifting of seats all around.

"He's going for the girl?" one of the elders asked.

Barbara paused then nodded. "I believe so."

"And tonight—"

"She's stronger than we thought." Barbara cut them off, frowning deeply. "It will make the payoff extraordinary, but the battle will be quite difficult."

The table remained silent, the room growing darker, as their auras delved into some blacker place. "If Jeremiah gets to her first—"

"He won't. He can't." Barbara took in a deep breath through her nose and let it out slowly. "If Jeremiah gets Charlotte before we do, we all die."

And to that, no one else seemed to find an appropriate response.

Chapter 18

Gabe was suffocating her. Charlotte knew she couldn't be annoyed, she had no right to be, so she bit her lip when he stood with her and followed her into the kitchen and held her tongue when he watched her make a sandwich for the two of them and didn't eat his until he was sure she was done. God, and she hadn't even asked to see the bodies of the rogues yet. She could only imagine how he would react to the inquiry.

"Don't you have work to do?" Charlotte sighed, leaning against the counter.

They had moved to a house closer to the center of town, seeing as wolves had made it inside Gabe's house twice now, nearly taking Charlotte's life with them both times. It was smaller, and less lived in. It seemed... stale.

"I am doing work," Gabe responded, tilting his head to the side to regard her. "Am I bothering you?"

"Yes."

He frowned.

"You've got about a thousand guys watching this house and the perimeter, Gabe. You're watching me as though I'm the enemy and suddenly, I'll turn into a wolf and bite into my own neck."

He grimaced and sat up straighter in his chair. "I'm restless. I can't leave you alone, not even if you asked me to. Inside, t-the beast, he can't leave."

Feeling foolish now, Charlotte dropped her arms and moved around the counter, feeling a burning tug in her chest demanding contact with him, demanding a connection.

He turned in his chair so Charlotte could step between his legs and lean in, resting her cheek on his chest. His hands came up almost instantly, cupping the back of her head and kneading the muscles at the back of her neck.

"I'm sorry. I know you're worried."

He was silent for a long moment. "I should be the one who's sorry."

She pulled back and met his blue eyes. "What do you mean?"

He took a strand of orange hair and pulled it from her face, brushing his thumb over a freckled cheek as he went. "My entire life, even when I was a child, I'd always believed that well…" He let out a huge breath, frustrated he couldn't find the right words. "I thought the wandering of the beasts was… normal. Natural. It was for our sanity and survival and was agreed by both of our ancestors. But… it doesn't seem right anymore."

Her eyebrows came together in confusion. "Shouldn't I be the one making you feel bad about this?"

He let out another monstrous sigh. "And you would be if you hadn't bit me. Your mind would be clearer. Remember how furious you were when I first brought you here?"

"You saved my life." She pointed out.

"And I should have brought you back afterward."

She shook her head in exasperation and took a step back. "I don't understand where this is coming from."

"This is coming from the fact that you were safe your entire life until I brought you here. Now, suddenly your grandfather is free and is coming after you. Do you not find that a little suspicious?"

She took another step back, feeling a burn in her calf where an angry red line remained from the claw mark. Her head hurt, trying to think clearly. Was it just because of her bite that she felt this way, felt so clouded from her own thoughts? Why didn't she miss her mother, the one who thought she was dead and the one who Charlotte had thought would hear her last words over the phone while she bled out among the remains of her car. Why didn't she miss her twerp of a brother, her brute of a dad, and her dog for crying out loud? Why did she feel... nothing?

She rubbed her temples, growling at herself. "What's happening to me?"

Gabe paused for a moment before answering. "Your body and mind are readjusting. You relied on family and past connection in your life and now... now, your body just needs me."

Why was she not angry at that? Gabe had stolen her from home, kept her from her family, yet she couldn't find it in herself to find anything wrong with him being the only important thing in her life.

She was sick.

"A-and if you don't connect back to me? If you can't complete that bond?"

Gabe shook his head, and Charlotte bit down hard on her lip, feeling a new ache in her chest, one hinting at how painful it will become the longer they went on like this. Only Charlotte was connected to Gabe, and that shouldn't be like that forever.

She cleared her throat and turned away so he couldn't see the tears stinging her eyes. She heard him move, the air shifting as he stepped up behind her, although when he touched her shoulder gently, she jerked and took a step forward out of reach, feeling terribly confused and torn in a hundred different directions.

"I need to see the bodies," she announced, still not facing him.

He was silent besides his steady breathing. She could feel the war within him, the struggle to reach out to her, his own pain. Her chest tightened further.

He cleared his throat. "Why?"

"They might have hidden runes beneath their fur or something else to tell me who did it specifically or their plans. Anything."

Another short silence. "Alright. I'll bring you over now."

She waited for him to turn first before steeling her resolve and following.

As rogues, their human minds were mostly gone, replaced by their beasts. They were natural pack animals, surviving off a community, an Alpha, and of authority. Without it, they lose their human side and give into the beast.

When they died, they stayed as the beast, ratty, dirty, and terribly, terribly sad.

That was what Charlotte stared at now, at the dead beast lying on the morgue's table with their glassy eyes open and fur matted with blood. Charlotte swallowed heavily, feeling Gabe's powerful presence just behind her.

"When you need to leave, just tell me," he said quietly.

She nodded stiffly and stepped closer to the dead beast. She wore gloves, and they felt like plastic on her fingers as she started parting the brownish-gray fur.

Odin stepped forwards, wearing his own set of gloves. "What are we looking for?" he asked.

"Any sort of rune."

"What would it look like?"

Charlotte shrugged, fighting back a wave of nausea as she searched the dead body. "It could look like anything. If you see something, no matter how small, that looked like something out of the ordinary, point it out. I'd rather tell you it's nothing a hundred times than miss something once."

He nodded, and they began their search while Gabe worked on another body behind them. They were silent other than the hum of florescent lights above them and the occasional gag Charlotte couldn't lock away.

"How about this?" Odin asked, parting some fur. Charlotte shook her head, and Odin went back to looking.

"Charlotte? What about this?" Gabe asked behind her. She walked over and peeked around his arm. She avoided the massive, fatal bite mark and focused on the blood splatter Gabe was pointing to. There was another shake of her head.

If she was lucky, there wouldn't be any other runes at all. Runes missed meant an entire day that power had gone unnoticed.

"This?" Odin asked, parting the fur with two hands by the beast's chest. Charlotte's eyes flickered up, saw the claw mark, and shook her head.

Then she paused.

Then her chest seized.

"Wait," she whispered, and immediately, Odin went back to the spot, to the cut in the beast's skin that she had thought was a battle wound.

It was so tiny, so unnoticeable that any other person would have missed it. Anyone other than Charlotte, who had been trained so thoroughly for things like this.

Gabe came to her side, feeling the shift in the air as Charlotte moved around the table, gently moving Odin aside so she could get a better look.

"I don't understand," she muttered to herself, eyebrows coming together.

"What? What is it?" Gabe prodded. Warriors crowded the doorway of the room, those watching over their king and queen, those anxious for news of their safety.

"It's like a combination of runes," she mumbled. "It's got a signature on it. I don't... I've never actually seen this before. I mean, it just confirms the fact an elder sent them. But I don't think—"

"What? You don't think what?" Odin said, feeling anxious and paranoid.

"I don't think it's my granddad."

Gabe hesitated before asking, "Can you be sure?"

She nodded, fighting the urge to rub her scar. "He drew his signature in my blood the night he tried to kill me. I won't ever forget it. This looks almost like him, but it's not."

"Who is it?" Odin asked. "What's it mean?"

She shook her head. "It's hard to distinguish them from each other. Signatures and actual runes are usually so tied in, no one can actually read it. Just give me a second."

Despite the canvas, Charlotte went back to all of her training, tracing her finger on the tiny, tiny incision on the dirty skin beneath the fur. It was so familiar.

Quite suddenly, her head whipped down to her leg, to the angry red mark still burning. "Oh, no," she said. The panic has not set in yet as her logical side worked through exactly what had been done. "Oh, no."

Gabe peeled his gloves off and grabbed onto Charlotte. "What? Charlotte, what is it?"

She pulled herself away, peeled her own gloves off, and started pacing the length of the tiny, cold room. "Just give me a second to think," she said absentmindedly.

"You've got to clue us in, baby," Gabe begged.

"It's in my blood," she hissed, running her hands through her hair and finally feeling the panic settle in. "It's in my freaking *blood*."

"What?"

"The *rune*, Gabe! The rune is in my own blood. It's flowing in me. There's no way to leak it out, no way to filter out that sort of power! Oh, god, they got me good. They got me really, really good. They weren't trying to kill me when they came in. The cut to my calf was all they really needed."

She shook her head, dazed and scared out of her freaking mind.

When Gabe opened his mouth to ask the next question, she shook her head, her stomach rolling, and answered him before he could speak. "It's going to tear apart my mind. The first thing the elders teach you is how important the mind is. The soul gives you power, the body gives you substance, and the mind connects the two. Without the mind, the soul can break free with nothing to hold it down."

"But your soul is locked," Gabe argued quickly. "Your grandmother locked it."

"How do you think they would ever unlock it? They could take another extra month to carefully remove that lock in my mind, and it would have the same result. This rune just destroys me completely. It'll take... God, it'll only take a week, tops."

Gabe took two big strides, stopping in front of her and grabbing her arms so she stopped too. "Who?" he demanded. "Who did this? Whose signature is that?"

The heat from his palms, his close proximity, and even his smell wrapped around her and forced her to calm down slightly, to regain a little control of her trembling limbs. How could she have ever hated this man?

"I don't know," she admitted. "It looks like my granddad's, but... it's not. Some pieces are different. I don't know who else it could be, though."

"Can he change his signature?"

"Not that I know of."

"But it could be possible?"

She paused then shrugged. Odin stood quietly by the door. "I don't know. Maybe. I never learned a lot about signatures."

Gabe let out a slow breath and brushed his palm down the side of her face, wondering if his precious mate would ever catch a break, would ever find peace.

"So... so you'll go mad?"

She nodded slowly. "Yes. That and worse. My mind will completely unravel and untangle until there's nothing left. Worse than going mad."

Her mind? Gone? He would never let that happen.

He would rather lose his own life first.

"Let's get out of this room," he announced, and she nodded, agreeing with a pained look in her eyes. "Let's figure this entire mess out."

Another nod, this one holding so much exhaustion, he was scared she might just collapse on the spot.

Chapter 19

She felt Gabe's hands on her shoulders as she stared off the front porch towards the rising sun. Staring for too long, the clouds changed, morphed before her green eyes, and changed into impossible shapes until she closed her eyes tight and told herself it wasn't real, it wasn't real, it wasn't *real*...

"How are you feeling?" His voice was soft, like a caress, and she relaxed as his fingers kneaded into the tense muscles of her neck when Gabe came up behind her.

"Fine," she lied fluidly. He sighed and walked across the porch until he could turn and lean against the railing, arms crossed over his chest.

"You look tired," he noted, eyes skirting over her face, frown lines creasing his perfect skin.

She tore her eyes away from him and back towards the sky. She hadn't slept in two days. Her dreams were plagued by terrible things. Her usual nightmares of her granddad were morphed now, changed so that he didn't just stab her but talked to her, telling her how much he hated her and how she ruined his life. She couldn't sleep. She refused to, not so she could just listen to things like that.

"How long do you think until you go crazy?" he asked.

Her eyes flickered to his, surprised by how straightforward the question was. His face was still lined with concern, giving nothing away. Charlotte swallowed then looked away once more. "I don't know."

But judging from how stressed her mind already was, she had to guess it was just a few more days until she tries to catch her own imaginary tail.

"Why do you think your granddad is making this so complicated?" he continued, not catching the hint that Charlotte just wanted to watch the sunrise quietly.

"Complicated?" she asked, scratching at the burning in her calf.

He shrugged and pushed off the railing so he could shove his hands into the pockets of his jeans. "I mean, he's a powerful guy. I bet you he could waltz right into the house and stab you in the heart again if he wanted."

She stared as though he had slapped her, shifting in her seat so she could stare at him wide eyed. He wasn't looking at her anymore, though. Instead, he was strolling across the porch to the other end, glancing around casually.

"Excuse me?"

He turned then, catching her green eyes with his blue ones. "Come on, Charlotte. He could kill you a thousand different ways. Why this backward route?"

"B-because my soul would be trapped inside my dead body. Technically, I couldn't die until my soul is unbound. Why are you asking these questions like that?"

"Like what?" he laughed humorlessly. "I'm asking it like it is, Charlotte. Your granddad tried killing you when you were a kid because he couldn't stand you, and now he's come to finish the job. What did you do to make him hate you so much?"

Charlotte's mouth hung open, eyes wide, her mind blank. A deep pain bloomed in her chest like Gabe was stabbing her right where her granddad had. Only Gabe was twisting the knife agonizingly slowly. She shook her head, having no response.

"I only ask because it's a matter of time before you either go insane or I figure it out myself. I don't want to be blindsided when it becomes clear that you just can't be loved, Charlotte."

"Gabe—"

"Do you think *I* could ever love you?"

He moved closer, head tilted and eyes glowing.

"*Stop.*"

"Do you think I could ever love you like you thought your granddad loved you? Because I'm having doubts."

That knife dug just a bit deeper and stung just a bit more. "What the hell, Gabe—"

"I don't think anyone could love you," he said, the final nail in the proverbial coffin. Charlotte's breath caught in her throat, her heart skipping a painful beat. "I don't think anyone could love you once they look past your façade to the damaged, scarred girl inside."

An odd, strangled sound erupted from her throat. Her hands came up and pushed at Gabe's chest, and he moved easily, as though he weighed no more than paper. Charlotte's hair whipped about her head and got caught on her cheeks as she fled across the wooden porch. She felt something snap and tear inside of her. She felt the world tilt at an entirely new, dangerous angle.

"Charlotte?"

She paused at the steps of the porch and turned quickly to face the doorway of the house. Gabe stood there, wearing a simple gray t-shirt and jeans and looking at her with equal parts confusion and concern. "Are you alright?"

Her head snapped to the side, but the other Gabe wasn't where she had pushed him away. He wasn't even wearing the same clothes as the Gabe before her.

"Oh, god," she moaned, pressing the heels of her hands against her closed eyes, trying to catch her breath. It wasn't real. None of it was real, yet the pain in her chest grew and blossomed with a life of its own.

He had no idea what the hell was going on, but Gabe gathered Charlotte into his arms regardless when she started shaking and carried her back in the house.

It was still warm outside during the day, but a fire burned in the living room regardless, crackling and heating the small space. It helped calm Charlotte and lulled her to sleep, and Gabe watched her silent form sprawled on the couch from his own chair across the room while he slowly burned to death.

She mumbled in her sleep. Her lips were moving, speaking, begging, and crying as her head turned to the side and her legs curled up into her body so she was more secure. He watched her carefully, feeling a crater erupt in his chest.

Charlotte was going mad.

Her grandad was trying to kill her.

Her mind was trying to kill her.

And Gabe was just watching everyone else try to do so.

There were things he didn't understand, too. Well, most things about Charlotte he didn't understand, like why her grandad stabbed her in the first place. As far as Charlotte told Gabe, he had helped train her for nine years before he went crazy and attacked her. He loved her and did everything with her.

And after the first failed attempt, why escape? Why now? And why go after his Charlotte again? For what purpose could her death serve?

What exactly was that ever elusive council really preparing Charlotte for? Certainly, not a spot on the council. She was far too young, far too inexperienced, and they never once taught her any of their laws or ways, just their runes.

He shook his head from his seat in the corner, rubbed a hand down his tired, haggard face, and focused his eyes on his mate's fiery hair. Like how the fire in the hearth calmed Charlotte, the fire glowing in her hair soothed Gabe.

She cried out softly, eyes screwing tightly shut, and Gabe's name was whispered with a sigh, drifting across the room like a desperate plea. He stood almost instantly, moving to the long couch before the furnace. He lifted her gently to not wake her—she hadn't slept in days, and he didn't want to ruin her precious moments of rest—and sat on the couch. When she was lowered one more, her head rested on his knees, and his hands smoothed away her wild, untamed hair, tracing lines on her face and soothing her with his touch.

Her soundless pleas died on her lips, and she became limp in his hold, finally, *finally* falling into the peaceful sleep she had been denied for so long.

Staring into the fire, Gabe nodded to himself, feeling a terrible sense of failure as he made a decision.

He didn't know what was happening to Charlotte. He had no idea how to stop her and her seemingly imminent death.

That meant he had to go to the people who knew just a bit more than he did. That meant leaving Charlotte in her grandmother's arms because the beasts couldn't roam the streets during the day.

But it meant helping her, he told himself. He didn't know what to do, so he needed to find the people who did.

And to save Charlotte, he would do anything.

Chapter 20

There were several things wrong on this particular night. Something was in the air.

It could have been the moon, cut at only half, yet shining as bright as if it were full. It could have been the billion something odd stars speaking to each other in Morse, winking in and out. Maybe it was in the air, the scent that had no odor, the sensation that had no texture. Just a feeling.

Or maybe, possibly, it was on that boundary that couldn't be seen… the boundary that encompassed the king of beasts and all his beastly subordinates. The boundary that wrapped around each town the elders built from the lumber they cut down all those years ago. The boundary the rogues couldn't pass beyond, and the one only Charlotte and the elders seemed capable of moving across.

Where, if you took a magnifying glass, you could tell not a single thing lived; not a blade of grass, not a curve of a tree root, not a spec of bacteria or fungus. There was nothing.

Like the black matter between stars, there was a peculiar... emptiness about the boundary around an energy fault.

But if you took a different sort of magnifying glass, one seen through a rune and the sharp eyes of an age-old elder, then you would also be able to see the hair thin fractures splintering through the boundary. You could see the cracks rise and erupt with each passing moon cycle, the boundary trembling as though something, somehow, was trapped within and pressing against that curious wall for release.

On this night, the elder on watch looked on in hopeless despair as the splinters scattered and moved about like greedy fingers to cover the surface of the boundary. And right there, right by that fly that couldn't figure out why it couldn't fly forwards anymore, right by that pinprick smaller than a nerve ending, something from within broke out, and leaked into the night on the other side. If you could see it leaking out, like the elder did with a cry of despair, then you could certainly feel it also like a bullet packed with heroin ripping through your heart, equal parts exhilarating and excruciating... like the very force keeping you alive was escaping through a tiny, tiny break in the wall.

Maybe, possibly, that could be what was wrong with this night.

How about the restless waves unsettling the tiny, unknown town filled with beasts? The town that followed a king with something more than just blind devotion. They followed their beastly king with so much dedication, they would lay down their lives so he could live another minute of his. They would give him the breaths from their very lungs if they thought it would allow him to smell the morning dew he loved so much just a little better.

The problem, though, if you must find one, lies in the same dedication that ruled the town. When there is no questioning of a single man with all power, then there is no questioning of his demise, either. And when the townspeople were willing to give everything for this one man, this one beast that rules them all, then they can't tell when it stops being for the good and ends up adding to the destruction of an entire town.

Because on that night, with that oddly bright moon shining, a boy hit puberty, and suddenly from within, a beast came ripping through, nearly tearing him apart from the inside out. And little Jason screamed because he couldn't quite remember anything being so painful before in his entire life.

That something else in the back of his head suddenly had life. It suddenly had a purpose, and it wanted out. It wanted out bad, but it was taking longer than usual… hours longer, excruciating, screaming, blistering hours longer than it should. They were hours where Jason's mom couldn't soothe him and his dad couldn't give him the right advice… hours where the healer started sweating for the first time in three hundred years because, well, she didn't know what was happening either.

They were hours where half the town howled to the moon for help and the other half that couldn't howl cried for their king to come, But the king of beasts didn't arrive because tonight, he was somewhere else.

On this night, when there's a blissful moment of pure, painless nothing, Jason becomes the beast. Panting, ears twitching, smaller than most but that's okay because he was sill just a kid hardly older than fourteen—he bit his mom.

She was just soothing him. She had two other boys, and physical contact soothed them after their first shift. It always had, and should have again, but this time, the smaller than average beast on the ground pulled a lip back, revealing sharp, glistening teeth. While his mom mumbled soothing words close to his head, those same teeth turned, sliced across her wrist, and clamped onto her jaw.

On this night, for the first time in hundreds of years, longer than anyone had been around, a new beast didn't feel the support of a pack around him after his first shift. For the first time, a beast is born rogue.

Maybe that was what's wrong with this night.

But then again, maybe the two women standing on the front porch was the most important cause... After all, it made the king of beasts pause on the edge of the forest as he was leaving as though this was a bad idea, a very, very bad idea. It was like the world right then, right at that moment, was speaking directly to him and telling him it was wrong. This was wrong.

This was a bad idea.

Gabriel, this is a terrible, terrible idea, the cosmos told him.

But how? How could a grandmother holding onto the shaking form of her granddaughter be a bad idea? How could giving his Charlotte the only hope he had be a bad idea?

But the sun was coming up, and the beasts could only roam the streets at night. No matter the effort involved in fighting the force tugging him back to his own town, the king of beasts was powerless. He had to leave the fiery-haired beauty on that porch even with the world screaming at him not to. He had to leave his Charlotte with nothing more than a promise to return the following night the moment he is allowed and a prayer to the moon battling the sun above that she still remembers who he was when he arrives.

Maybe that was what was wrong with the night.

And maybe the next night, the one after that, and the others after that would only be so much worse.

Maybe something big was happening, and everything inside of that energy fault line, trapped within the boundary, was about to feel it.

Chapter 21

It was raining outside.

No, raining was the wrong word. It was a never-ending deluge, a rain so brutal, you would drown by stepping off your front porch. The trees and grass were brutalized, the leaks in the roof were spreading, and all living things were seeking what little shelter they could find.

It was early morning, not that you could tell. The clouds blocked all light and allowed the shadows to wander wherever they pleased though where the child crouched in the corner, blood smeared, pale skin trembling, not even the shadows were brave enough to be near.

When the king of beasts arrived with matted fur and an itching feeling of disaster in his chest, he was met with blood soaked mud and a town in shambles. He was swarmed the moment he was noticed by those on four like him and those on two. Women were crying, and others shouting. The men were telling him too many things at once, beasts howling and growling.

There was pandemonium, none of which he could understand over the damn rain.

Good old Odin, though, his highest friend among all his friends, his second in command, was able to pull him to the side, offering him a pair of shorts and a brief, somber explanation.

Jason changed. Jason changed wrong. Jason's mother was fighting to keep another breath in her chest in the healer's house.

And now, Jason was in some corner, too fragile for anyone to come close to him without endangering himself or others.

From his vantage point, Gabe could see the blockade of beasts blocking Jason if he decided to run but moving no closer.

"How long?" Gabe asked. The rain pelted down and dripped into his eyes.

"His shift took five hours. When he got his mind back enough, the reality of what he did to his mom drove him back to madness. He has been like this for three hours now."

Gabe gritted his teeth and flexed his jaw. That beast within him was stirring, rising up, and threatening to take control in a beastly way. His town was in distress, a member of his pack was in shambles, and it was his duty, in his very nature and coded into his own damn genes, to do something.

He strode across the mud on bare feet, the rain and his beasts parting to allow him a path to the small boy in the corner of the house. Thoughts of Charlotte faded to the back of his mind... thoughts of her death, of the imminent future without her before him, and thoughts of what the hell the point of anything was dissipated.

All because this was his town, his pack, and they have been for hundreds of years. These people, beasts or not, were deeper than family and stronger than friends. They were life, connection, everything.

And one of them was rogue. One of them was born rogue. It was his job to protect and defend these people, and he would until his very last breath.

He stepped close enough so Jason could feel his presence like the raw power it was. He stopped trembling and froze up to the point of pain, but he didn't turn.

"Face me," Gabe demanded. All other beasts faced him and stood with their backs straight, heads held high, proudly awaiting a command even though knowing it wouldn't be directed at him. All beasts did but the boy before the king. "Face me."

"Stop it, stop it, stop it," he said quietly, a small chant on his pale lips. His head twitched and shook like he could shake off the pull to do as Gabe bid. The disease in his head, the madness, was taking hold, making him see red and nothing but. It was red like mom's roses, like her blood when he bit her.

Gabe was well versed in commanding those in his town, those who recognized him as the leader, as the king of beasts. He was well versed in handling those who became rogues when they challenged his status, but he wasn't well versed in creating a pack member from someone born outside, though.

He was, though, among all other things, a king. He was the king of all beasts, and authority ran in his blood.

"Jason."

The boy flinched, his name hitting him like a slap. It wasn't that it was demanded of him to stand and face the voice of authority behind him. It wasn't that his name was laced with a thousand levels of command and authority, leaving no room or argument.

It was from the fact that Gabe, a man standing tall and proud as the king of beasts, had called his name so softly as nothing more than someone ready to offer support in a time of severe need.

And when he turned around with his sopping brown hair matted to his forehead, he blinked at his king, kneeling before him and feeling his bottom lip tremble. He couldn't help it, not even when he tried. Men shouldn't cry, he knew that. Dad had said there was no shame in crying, but Jason never saw Gabe shed a tear.

Yet at that moment, cold, tired, and feeling the fogginess leave his mind with a headache in its wake, he couldn't help it.

"I'm... I'm sorry." He hiccupped. "I didn't mean it."

Gabe held his eyesight and nodded his head once. "It's alright, Jason. You're going to be alright."

Because he was already crying and there was no taking that back, he didn't see much wrong from scrambling to his feet and latching onto Gabe. There wasn't much wrong in his head with hiding his face from the beasts watching him until they were in the warmth of a house with a towel wrapped around his body and his dad ushering him towards a fire.

Gabe, on his own once more, had nothing left to do but figure out what in the actual hell was going on and who would go rogue next.

And right on the edge of the woods, where a man became the shadows, where he carried no scent and no presence, just a figure amongst the darkness, a set of sea-green eyes watched the progression through the rain. The timing would be just right when *he* steps from the shadows for the first time in years.

"Grandma, I don't feel good."

She could still feel him. She could still feel Gabe as though he were beside her. She could feel every brutal emotion he felt. Hell, she could feel his soul coursing through her own veins, making her ache with the need to let him see her own.

"You'll feel better soon, honey. I swear," her grandma promised, humming to herself in tune with the pounding rain outside.

With her eyes closed, Charlotte could very nearly feel her mind splitting apart. Like a rot, it spread through every thought, wiping her memories piece by piece. If she thought real hard, she could remember her brother's eyes were green just like hers. If she thought even harder, she could remember falling down the stairs when she was seven.

But no matter how hard she thought, she couldn't remember what she got for her birthday last year. She couldn't remember what Gabe had made her for dinner the other night.

The image of her mother in her memories was fading, and the sound of her dog's bark sounded muffled. Things were falling apart.

A cramp formed in her leg, reminding her she was sitting on the floor. Why was she on the floor? She couldn't remember, couldn't remember what was happening anymore. Grandma said it was alright, that she would be alright, and as the thought circulated around her head, she felt herself drifting back into that peaceful place in her head once more.

She opened her eyes, catching sight of charcoal on the ground. Her head ached from the light, yet it was raining outside, dark from the clouds. Why was it so bright? "Grandma, I don't feel…"

Her voice faded, her head was swimming, and her eyes were closing. When she opened them next, she was more focused, and she grew more confused at the runes surround her, more confused as to why she was sitting on the floor in her grandma's living room in the center of a circle of charcoal drawn runes.

"Grandma?" she asked, panicking. Runes like these weren't used for fun. She could feel it connecting to her and taking something important. "Grandma!"

"Hush, sweetheart. You're alright. I'm trying to help, you've got to keep quiet." Charlotte saw her leaning over an old book on the table, reading glasses perched at the end of her nose. Her strawberry blonde hair looked dull, flat, and graying at the ends and splitting. Her skin was sagging and aging, and Charlotte couldn't remember her grandmother ever looking so much like a grandmother before.

Her eyes darted over the runes and felt her throat close. "Grandma, these runes—"

"I said hush, Charlotte," Her grandma snapped, turning her head to catch Charlotte's gaze with her own furious one. "Close your eyes again. You'll feel better soon."

"Oh, my god," she mumbled. Her heart was pounding like crazy, her head was spinning, and her mind was splitting. She looked at the rune on the floor and tried to stand but couldn't find the strength. "No, Grandma, you wouldn't—"

"Charlotte, sweetheart, you're making it very hard to concentrate." Her grandma sighed. "Hush, please. It's the last time I'll ask."

Panic bloomed in Charlotte's chest. As raw as it can be, she clawed at the wooden floors of her grandma's floor, trying to brush her hands over the runes to destroy them. Pain trailed up her arm upon contact, like a flare of agony. Gasping, she clutched her hand to her chest, trying to find strength, trying to find a way out.

Her grandma sighed and straightened from the book before grabbing her charcoal and stepping forwards. "Charlotte, honey, it won't be much longer, alright?"

"Grandma, please. I don't understand you said you'd help not to—"

"Charlotte!" her grandma snapped, closing her eyes tight and regaining her temper. When she opened her eyes, she was eerily calm, bending down to add another rune to the circle enclosing Charlotte. "It's going to be alright, honey, I promise. You'll feel as good as new when I'm done."

"I thought you couldn't hurt me," Charlotte said quietly, more shell-shocked than anything. "I'm... I'm Gabe's mate." This was her grandmother, wasn't it? The woman adding to the runes and pulling Charlotte's energy from her? The woman who helped raise her, nurture her, and saved her when her grandpa tried to kill her? Was this the same woman?

Her grandma looked up over her glasses, catching Charlotte's eye. "I'm not hurting you, Charlotte."

"You're k-killing me." She blinked, feeling groggy and exhausted. "You're h-hurting me."

Her grandma reached forward, ran a wrinkled hand down Charlotte's pale cheek, and tucked a red curl behind her ear. "No, sweetheart, I'm not." She sighed. "Freeing someone's mind won't hurt them, baby. Not when you're only helping the process along. I told you, you'll feel fine in just a little while, Charlie."

Not much else could be said, not when Charlotte felt her mind closing down once more, her eyes slipping shut. Not when there was no worries in the place Charlotte went, nothing but an ache in her gut and the sound of rain on the roof.

"Grandma..." She sighed, her chest constricting. "I don't feel too good."

And from the corner, where she was hunched over the table, her grandma pushed her glasses back up her nose and hummed in the back of her throat. "You'll feel better soon, sweetheart. I promise."

Chapter 22

She waited on the back porch for him, standing by the railing with her fingers and pulling at the hem of her shirt.

And she waited.

And waited.

The moon grew tall in the sky, the stars multiplied and dispersed, and Charlotte waited. Inside, something was clawing to the surface that made her skin itch. She wanted to run off the porch and into the woods to find Gabe and tell him—tell him what?

You couldn't see by looking at her, not with her face set in such a strict mask and her back as straight as it was, but Charlotte was tearing apart inside. She was forgetting everything at the same rate her mind was making things up. She couldn't remember where her house was in this town, yet somehow, she had sworn she spent hours this afternoon with Gabe despite the fact he physically couldn't enter the town during the day.

Yet it was as though her mind had forgotten something incredibly important, so important it had left a carbon copy behind so that as she stood on the porch waiting for her beast to come back to her, she fought her own mental decay to remember. Runes... she remembered runes, but her grandma had been using runes to help her all day long.

But there was something else... something more. Without knowing it, Charlotte raised her hand and rubbed her scar where it ached straight down to the organ beating beneath her chest. Where the hell was Gabe?

Like a bullet, an image of her on the ground, aching and losing her mind in a prison of runes, blinded her. She stumbled to the side, catching herself on the porch when it felt like her legs would give out. God! Oh, god. Oh, *god*. She straightened herself, suddenly begging for Gabe to arrive more than ever. Her grandma was killing her. Her goddamn grandma was goddamn *killing* her.

Heaving and trying to catch a breath, Charlotte took a step as though to run when the sound of the back door had her pausing.

And just like that, like the breeze represented inside her fragile mind, the thought of her grandma killing her was blown away. The woman stepping out onto the porch with her was not a murderer, but a friend, a second mother, someone Charlotte loved dearly.

She offered a smile and relaxed, wondering when she had gotten so tense. "Grandma," she greeted. "What are you still doing at this hour?"

Her grandma came to her side and then passed her, dropping into the chair by the back porch corner. "I don't sleep much anymore, sweetheart," she admitted, peeking up at the sky. "Where's your beast tonight, Charlie?"

Her purpose for being out there so late, so desperate, came back like a sobering punch. "I don't know." She shrugged and turned back to face the forest off her grandma's porch just in case Gabe decided to show up at that moment. "Grandma, why—" Charlotte winced, feeling foolish for being unable to ask a simple question.

"Why didn't I tell you about the beasts? About *us*?" Her grandma supplied for her, saving Charlotte from her moment of weakness.

Charlotte winced again but nodded. "I could have handled it. I just... I don't understand. Why lie? Why tell everyone the beasts are terrible, that they're, well, beasts? Why can I leave, but no one else can? Nothing makes sense."

Silence met Charlotte, but she waited. Her grandma taught her patience and stubbornness in equal parts. "Take a seat, Charlie."

She didn't move at first, and instead, stared harder into the darkness around her. When Gabe didn't show in a flurry of perfect timing, she turned and sat beside her grandma. There was another bout of silence. Her grandma was always one for theatrics, for burning the minutes until anticipation was almost deadly.

"You and I are extraordinary creatures." Her grandma sighed. She lifted an aged and wrinkled hand and examined the effects of time catching up. "What we do is the finest of arts. We discover and manipulate that thin line between miracle and madness."

Charlotte nodded, scratching her scar absentmindedly when it burned. She had heard this a thousand times as a kid. In every lesson, the same speech was given. "Why keep the beasts so secret, though? Why did you have to make us fear them?"

"Because they need their mates, Charlotte, and a family isn't giving their child over to a bunch of beasts willingly."

"You don't know that."

"I do. We tried. For the first few decades, we tried until the townspeople stormed the beasts for their loved ones. It was a near massacre of our people. There was no other way."

Charlotte closed her eyes and tried to stop imagining that. "But fault lines?" She pressed for more information. "Energy fault lines? A-and only us can leave? Grandma, did you sign a... a contract a long time ago? Something to trap everyone here?"

Her grandma grinned suddenly, a giggle escaping. "Trapped?" she looked at Charlotte with an eyebrow raised. "Oh, Charlotte, they're not trapped."

Charlotte knew better than to question her grandma further, that she would tell her more only when she felt like it. Then again, Charlotte also knew that her mind was burning to the ground and this small moment of sanity wouldn't last. She didn't have time for patience anymore.

"Grandma, please—"

"We need a fault line to survive." She cut in, voice sharper than it has been. "When it is in our nature to pour energy out of ourselves consistently every time we use a rune, there is no other way to live than by a source. Outside of one, we can survive maybe a week. Inside, we can survive for much longer."

"How much longer?"

To that, her grandma pursed her lips and gazed out to the shadows Charlotte had spent hours looking in. "Until that energy fault breaks, Charlie. Until we've stayed so long that there's no more energy left to use."

"And then what? What happens to us, to all the people afterward? To my mom and dad and brother? They're not like us. They're not like you or the elders. Why are they wrapped up in all of this too?"

Annoyed now, completely lacking her cool and calm exterior, her grandma turned her head to the side and fixed Charlotte with a withering glare. "When you settle on a fault lie, you lock it. No external energy recycling happens. If we can't die, then we need to feel the line from somewhere."

"You settled those people here with you just so they could die? Just so they could give their energy, their souls, to the fault line and let you live?"

Appalled, Charlotte stood up. Her heart was beating fast, and now, just as before, certain memories came to the forefront, sprinkled with fear, panic, and a different kind of pain.

Her grandma stood with her, looking older and more fragile than ever under the moonlight. "The world isn't roses and sunshine, sweetheart. The world's about surviving. This is what we do. This is who we are."

"Then... then why are you killing me too?" Charlotte asked, even as the memories flickered like a loose light bulb, reminding her and making her forget in seconds of who her grandma really was. It was exhausting standing there, fighting madness even though it was like fighting a bush fire with a water gun.

"Charlie," her grandma said, more herself, calm, and sincere. She took a step towards Charlotte, who countered it with one of her own. She was powerful, more powerful than Charlotte, and she had no idea what kind of runes and tricks her grandma had lying around. She needed out. *Get away*, her mind screamed. *Get away. Get away. Get away...*

"Your beast isn't here, honey," she said, almost sadly, with a shake of her head. "He's preoccupied someplace else and will be for a while. No one is coming to save you. No one is coming for you at all. This is just the way it has to be."

Her grandma took another step, and Charlotte stumbled back once more. "The energy fault is breaking, isn't it?" she asked, blinking and trying desperately to fight a losing battle. *Stay sane,* she told herself. *Stay sane. Get out. Find Gabe. Stay sane.* "And you're dying."

Her grandma paused, tilting her head to the side as her graying strawberry blonde hair fell to the side. "I'm not dead yet, Charlotte."

Her next step forward, Charlotte didn't remember, not when despite her best efforts, her mind slipped once more, and she faded away into nothingness.

Gabe lifted his head and stared at the sun high in the sky until his eyes burned. That damn thing seemed to be stuck at its highest point. He itched and ached to find Charlotte. The human knew he had nothing left to offer, no way to help her, but the beast didn't care.

Gabe needed her.

It is what she needs, he told himself. It is what she needed.

He was on his roof, leaning back on the black tiles. The sun was high, yet the roof felt cool to the touch, almost pleasant to lean on. His eyes skirted over the sky, passed over each cloud, and followed every bird. Why did Charlotte always stare up when she was up here? It was boring. He has been there since sunrise, and after the burst and swirl of color, it has been absolutely dull.

Would he ever find out what she watched when she came up to the roof and watched the sky? Why she did it?

Gabe knew several things about Charlotte. He knew she was brilliant, but that was obvious. You could tell in the way he looked at things like it was all a puzzle and her only goal was to put it together. She could spend hours staring at the tree tops and pulling Gabe to her side with something akin to childlike excitement just to tell him how photosynthesis works.

He also knew Charlotte wasn't perfect. For him, she was the most perfect thing in the world, but reality would disagree. She had allergies, and when her nose ran after sneezing seventeen times, she would rub it on her sleeve then do some sort of chunky sniffle thing.

There was also this thing she did when she woke up in the morning, without fail, every single day. She sat up, blinked like she was drugged, then stretched, but it wasn't a normal stretch. That he wouldn't mind. It was break her spine, reach for the sun, go into a split sort of stretch. And not even that, he would mind. It was the screech she did while stretching that made his ears bleed. She was perfect, he swore it, but Charlotte could hit pitches not even his beast could hear.

Charlotte was naturally compassionate, though. She didn't have to try. She didn't have to put in a single ounce of effort. It was just in her blood. The small things she did, like opening the windows when she woke before him because she knew he liked the smell of morning dew or speaking to the kids in town because she knew they looked up to her, couldn't go unnoticed. She was perfect.

There was plenty of things he still didn't know about her, too, and that was an awful thought. With a whole life having Charlotte beside him, he would have made it a challenge to discover every little thing.

But now, he might never find out what she looked at up on this roof.

She was also miles away, and the day was dragging on and on and on.

"Gabriel," Odin called from the front yard, head craned back to gaze up at his king. "Jason's gone."

"Did you check the shed again?" He sighed. The boy had fled there hours earlier, upset to tears again. The town had been in a flurry finding him until someone heard the sniffles from the shed in the backyard.

"We've checked everywhere," Odin said. Gabe noticed the twinge of unease in his voice for the first time, "and his scent fades into the forest."

Gabe swore, leaping from the roof and landing feet beside his friend. "No one went after him?"

Odin paused. "We thought with Charlotte's granddad out—"

"He's after Charlotte, not us."

"And Charlotte fell in love with a beast." Odin was quick to argue. "What better way to get to her than through us?"

Gabe grunted and started walking past Odin. "She doesn't love me." He sure as hell wished she did.

"Grab three others. Meet me out there," he called back over his shoulder to his friend before meandering his way through town. He met the edge of the forest, inhaled deeply, and let the beast within taste the air and catch Jason's scent.

The next moment, the shadows swallowed him up, and he was surrounded by the thick, heavy scent of nature. The only sound around him was the crunch of the leaves and sticks, snapping like gunshots in the still air.

For a moment, a sense of unease settled into Gabe's chest. Most animals fell silent around a beast's approach. It was instinct to do so upon a predator's arrival, but Gabe had incredible senses, and he could hear every animal before they heard Gabe.

If they were silent now... well, Gabe could only assume there was an even bigger predator around.

Instinct allowed his beast to take control of Gabe's actions, and it let his eyes see things differently in the foggy sunlight coming from the forest canopy and let that other sense taste the air for something bigger, something more dangerous than the king of beasts himself.

Jason's scent intensified, signaling he was closer, but Gabe nearly ripped the boys head off by accident when he stepped from around a tree, facing Gabe with trembling hands.

"Jesus, Jason," Gabe growled, tugging a hand through his hair. "You can't run off like this, kid. You've got the entire town out looking for you again."

Jason blinked slowly, staring at Gabe for a long moment. He blinked again before a spark of recognition flared life into the boy's eyes. "Gabe?" he asked, voice trembling.

Something wasn't right. Something really, really wasn't right.

"Jason—"

"It is you." He breathed out, smiling, stepping forwards, and reaching a hand out for Gabe. "I was so scared it was someone else."

"Someone else? Who?"

Jason smiled and lifted a trembling hand, and Gabe didn't see the symbol painted on his palm until it was too late... until Jason's hand was touching Gabe's exposed arm.

A jolt shot through Gabe's body like an extra thousand pounds was added to his build. Jason dropped almost instantly into a lifeless pile on the forest floor. If it weren't for the sound of his steady heartbeat, Gabe would have thought he was dead.

And he would have kneeled beside him, too, picked him up and darted back to town for help and backup if he could move at all. His limbs were stuck, frozen and limp beneath a terrible weight on every part of his body.

"The boy's fine, I can assure you," came a deep, tired voice from the shadows. Gabe's head jerked up just as a figure emerged from the protruding darkness of the forest, gray hair hanging around his old, aging face. "He's just a bit worn out. Beasts shouldn't use runes, after all, but I need all the energy I can."

"Jerimiah," Gabe hissed, a rage burning him up.

The old man grinned. It wasn't maniacal, it wasn't cruel, it was just a warm smile in greeting. "Gabe, how great it is to finally meet you. I've been waiting a while for the right time, but seeing as your mate seems to be running out of time, I'm running low on it also."

Gabe tugged against the frozen state of his body to no avail, his efforts going unnoticed. "What have you done to her?" He snarled, seeing red.

"Me?" Jerimiah laughed then threw his head back and just laughed to the sky. "I've done nothing yet. You, though… You've been fooled to the utmost degree, Gabriel."

He pulled a pocket knife from his khakis and strolled to a pine tree. If Jeremiah hadn't reached for it, Gabe would never have noticed the symbol carved into the bark. Jeremiah ran his knife through it, marring its perfection, and like a light switch, the day turned to night.

Gabe glanced around at the pitch black sky, his beast allowing him to see through the dark. Not even the moon seemed to be alive on this night. "What the hell is this?" Gabe hissed.

"It's night time, Gabe. Since you've dropped Charlotte off, it's been night, it's been day, and it's been night again, and you've sat around like an idiot the entire time, caught in a time loop." Jerimiah sighed and shook his head. "Barbara was always one for the intricate tricks."

Days? It's been *days*? "Barbara did this?"

"Oh, yes, and much more, but that's not what I need to talk to you about right now."

"Release me," Gabe demanded. "Release me, and we'll talk."

"Yes, I assume it'd be quite easy for you to talk to my mangled, deformed body." The old man laughed. "You'd kill me in an instant, no matter how much I insist that you hear what I'm going to say."

And damn it, he was right. Gabe knew a thousand different ways he wanted to kill the man. He could feel the need burning his blood.

"And what do you have to say?" Gabe forced himself to ask. Charlotte was in danger. Charlotte could be dead right this very second, and he was trapped in his own prison, unable to help.

Jerimiah leveled Gabe with an even stare, one that demanded attention, one that didn't leave room for a haughty argument. "Your mate's going to die, Gabriel. There's no getting around it."

Gabe snarled, the sound tearing through the still night. Profanities spewed from his mouth at a rate even Charlotte would be in awe of as he fought his own body to get his hands on the horrific man in front of him.

"Gabriel." Jerimiah snapped, and for a moment, the king of beasts paused, surprised by his own obedience. "Enough. Charlotte is going to die. There's no way around it, so you need to stop snarling like a wounded puppy and listen up."

"Why tell me this?" Gabe growled, his own rage burning him alive. "What purpose does this have?"

Jerimiah placed another one of his withering stares upon Gabe, pinning the beast in place.

"Because I'm going to kill your mate," he declared in a voice strong and firm, "and you're going to let me."

Chapter 23

Charlotte could hear the floor boards creak and feel the air shift as someone joined her in the room. Her head was lowered, her matted red hair looking more like a dull burn than the fire itself. Her eyes were closed, yet she remained awake despite being denied sleep for hours, days maybe. Going insane made it hard to keep time.

Finding a small sliver of energy within her, she managed to lift her head and open her eyes.

Gabe sat before her, cross-legged, his knees just centimeters from the edges of the runes. His blue eyes were glowing, and his head was cocked to the side.

"I know you're not real," Charlotte muttered but couldn't take her eyes off him. "I know you're not real."

He nodded his head while blinking slowly at her, and Charlotte's chest ached at just how beautiful he was, how perfect, despite the fact that he was just a figment of her imagination come to life. "Of course, I'm not real, Charlie. You're completely mad."

She found a small smile forming on her lips, one of pure exhaustion. "I've missed you." Her eyes stung. Were they tears? God, she missed Gabe. "Where... where have you been? I've been waiting, and you don't—You haven't shown up yet."

He lifted a broad shoulder then dropped it once more in a half shrug. "I'm not really Gabe, remember? I couldn't tell you."

"Aren't you going to tell me it's because you don't love me?" she asked in a small, hardly herself voice. "Aren't you going to tell me that I'm a monster, that you haven't come yet because this is easier for you?"

He rolled his eyes, making her heart leap in her chest. Every movement from him, no matter the mockery involved, made her heart beat faster and that ache hurt just a bit more. "I'm your thoughts manifested, Charlie. You know deep, deep down that I love you."

"You never said—"

"We didn't have to say it," he cut her off sharply. "We shouldn't base our relationship on spoken words. You know how I feel even if I didn't say it. You've seen into my own damn soul for crying out loud. You can't deny it."

And she couldn't, not when the manifestation of her thoughts was telling it to her directly.

God, she needed the real Gabe. He would get her out of this circle. He would save her, and if he couldn't... well, at least it would be nice to have someone there when she died.

"I would be really glad to spend the rest of my life with you," she muttered, choking on something in her throat. Her eyes burned, tears threatening to spill, but she could hardly care. She was tired. So very, very tired. "I know that sounds crazy. I mean, it should. I am crazy, but jeez, Gabe, please just be real. Please, Gabe, please be real. Please, please, please…"

"Charlotte." His voice was sharp, cutting her off from her rant and making the tears stop their downward track from her eyes even when she hadn't realized they had spilled over. "I'm not coming, and that means something's wrong. Think, Charlie. Your grandma knew I'd come for you. She probably has me locked down somewhere, or worse. You need to get out of here on your own because I'm not going to be able to do it for you. You're a brilliant person. Use what little you have left of that brain."

"I don't know."

"Think, Charlie!"

She started like he had slapped her, and in a moment of panic, her mind ran on full throttle for the first time in days. "I have no way to make a rune of my own," she said, shaking her head. "I'd have to break one of these, but I can't get close to them. There's an energy pushing back against me."

Without him saying anything, she knew he was asking for her gaze, and she offered it to him, meeting those magnificent blue eyes. "You can break the rune," he told her with his jaw tight. "You're stronger than them, always have been. It's why they're using you now. You *can* break the rune."

She was breathing hard as her eyes skirt over the black symbols on the floor. She could break it. She could do it. She could if she ignored the fact her very bones would crack before she got close enough to them to run a fingernail through the charcoal. But she could do it.

"You'll be sitting there when I do?" she asked, looking back up to see Gabe watching her.

"Probably not," he said. "You don't have many moments of sanity left. I'll be gone, and you'll probably forget this entire event altogether."

She swallowed but nodded her head. She was strong, and she could be strong for just a bit longer. "I'll be okay," she told Gabe and herself. "If you're not coming for me, then I'll come for you."

He paused then nodded his head, a smile tugging at the corners of his mouth. "That's my girl."

She was a ghost, drifting through the shadows in her long white shirt. She hadn't done a damn thing to herself, yet her hair seemed brighter than before. You could try, and you would fail, to catch her eye. They were everywhere at once, never where they were supposed to be.

She drifted like she was the darkness itself. Incorruptible and untouchable, you wouldn't be able to reach her, not in this state, not with her mind miles and miles away.

Deeper into the woods, further into its never ending darkness, she walked. Her feet bled, but she didn't feel it. Her hand ached where it was shattered, bled where the pieces of bone had broken her skin, but that ache belonged to a different part of her mind.

Her grandma would return in a few moments to find a scratched up rune and her granddaughter's blood on the floor where Charlotte had pressed against her prison of symbols until she reached the charcoal. Barbara would curse and move as fast as her frail body could to call upon those mad beasts who had helped her up to this point. She had gotten them to cut her leg all that time ago, got them to drive Charlotte mad, so maybe they could be useful once more.

It wouldn't be until Charlotte was deep enough in the woods, though, that her grandma wakes up and finds her gone. It wasn't until a pine cone embedded itself into Charlotte's heel that she snapped from the mindless trance she was in and looked around her, blinking slowly while catching up with her thoughts and letting the confusion catch up as well.

Because, as the imaginary Gabe had promised, she had forgotten everything that had happened while sitting in that circle of runes, and once again, she was alone. For just a while longer, just a few more hopeless hours more, Charlotte would be on her own.

And it wouldn't be until Charlotte's most hopeless moment that the king of beasts would catch her once more and hold onto her tightly this time.

Chapter 24

"If you had to choose between the life of your mate and the life of your entire pack, which would you choose?"

Jeremiah stood by the old oak where Barbara's rune was scratched out, leaning casually against the bark. He glanced up from his nails, where he picked at the dirt with his pocket knife, to cast Gabe a curious glance.

"No answer?"

Of course not. Of course, Gabe wouldn't answer a question like that, not while seething as he was, not while so incredibly furious that he felt like he could burn himself down to a pile of ashes right where he was. There was something especially brutal about staring a monster down without being able to take a single step.

"No, I wouldn't suppose you'd have an answer to that." Jeremiah shrugged a thin, bony shoulder and sighed. "Both are equally important. They hold an equal space in your heart and your soul. A pack, a mate, a life. How could I ask such a silly question?"

Jeremiah glanced up once more as if to see if Gabe was still listening like he had any other choice but to do so. He had no choice but to stand there frozen while Charlotte was probably being murdered that very second.

"You see, Gabe, the fault line is breaking." Gabe stiffened so slightly, you would have missed it if you were some other person, but Jeremiah wasn't just some other person. His lips quirked up into a half smile, the wrinkles on his face stretching. "Do I have your attention now, my king?"

Gabe snarled but fought to reign his beast in. He just had to wait. He didn't know a lot about runes, and he didn't know if Jeremiah could keep him in this spot for eternity if he so chose, but he damn well hoped not.

"Our dear beloved fault line is splitting apart at the seams. Has been for a little while now. It's always so sad when this happens, so utterly defeating. For my species, at least. Do you know what a fault line cracking means for me? For my people?"

He quirked an eyebrow, but Gabe offered no response. He just stood in his prison, crippled with unbridled rage.

"We die, Gabriel. The fault line breaks, and we die the very second it happens. Very peacefully and very painlessly, our souls will float away. It is our life cycle and our end." A look of foreboding so unlike Jeremiah came over the old man and made his face morph into a deep set frown. "There is something equally terrifying about it too. Can you imagine, Gabriel, knowing when you're going to die? Knowing you've lived for hundreds of years, and that it's all going to end quite suddenly?"

"That's what happens." Gabe snarled, his first words since Jeremiah started his rant. "People die."

Jeremiah made a savage smile, one that had even Gabe shivering. "Not if we can help it."

The frail man took a step, carefully moving away from a tree root. "See, a few centuries ago, we found a loophole... a brilliantly sadistic loophole. We lock ourselves to a land, but instead of throwing the key away, we took it with us. We kept it by our side until the fault line breaks, then we can get out of there, unscathed, with enough time to settle back down for another two or three centuries."

Gabe moved as though to lunge at the man, but of course, he was unable to do so. He was unable to move, save for a small twitch, a less than noticeable movement that flew by the all-seeing eyes of Jeremiah. Gabe felt it, though, the weight pressing him down shifting.

"You made Charlotte your key." He accused. "She's your way out."

Jeremiah showed his most humble face yet, his sea-green eyes darkening to a somber tone before he nodded. "God, help us, but we did."

"Either she lied, or she's two hundred years old. She can't be." Gabe argued, even with Jeremiah telling it right to his face.

"Certainly not." Jeremiah agreed. "You would have found her centuries ago if that were the case. Her soul is as old as she is."

"Then how—"

"Did you know that every time one of your beasts mated with a human from our town, it chipped away a piece from the fault line? Surprised? Why have you never heard of our kind sharing a land with yours? It weakens the line every time you mate."

"Why did you then?" Gabe seethed.

"Because we can grab onto those chips and store them until someone is born with a strong enough soul to latch them onto so will be alive when the fault line finally does break. The chips can't be used without a soul, without something to feed it. Otherwise, they lay dormant, unusable for years until they're put to use."

He paused, pursing his lips momentarily. "Imagine how much energy that person would have stored within them if the fault line was attached to their very soul? Imagine how much energy would be released if their soul was taken at the exact time the fault line broke apart?"

"Just about enough to keep you alive until you find the next fault line, I'd assume," Gabe said through gritted teeth, pressing against his boundary. He didn't care how Jeremiah and the elders discovered this loophole or how they knew this would work and keep them alive when every other settlement of their species died with the fault line like they should have. "You were going to rip the soul from your granddaughter's body to keep your pathetic ass alive."

"Yes, I was." He nodded his head, stoically hiding any sort of shame he might have felt, and Gabe certainly searched hard enough for it. "How's the pack doing, Gabe?"

The sudden question had Gabe pausing in his efforts to free himself from this frozen prison. "Excuse me?"

Jeremiah glanced at the unconscious boy on the forest floor. "He seemed a bit... mad, didn't he? What's the word I'm looking for? Rogue?"

Gabe snarled viciously. "What have you done?"

"Me? Nothing. You? You mated with a woman who could never complete the bond. I can think of no better way to destroy a pack than to deny it half a leader."

Instinct made it hard to process that newest piece of information. His defense mechanism unconsciously took the thought of destroying his pack by taking a mate and stored it in the back part of his mind where it wouldn't haunt him. The instinct to take that initial horror and bury it six feet deep was too strong. He had a beast, after all, and most beasts new no other detrimental emotion other than anger.

"We've lived centuries without a queen," he hissed.

"Because until you brought her to your pack, your soul and your heart was the only one they needed," Jeremiah hissed back just as violently, silencing the beast before him. "You hooked them to their queen, Gabriel. They don't know you as their king anymore without her. If Charlotte's soul remains alive, your pack will be destroyed. If she dies, her soul leaves, and you'll become the only thing your pack needs once more."

His snarls were a music of their own, each note a cry of the monster within his soul screaming in protest. "Is this your goal? Destroy Charlotte and my pack?"

"Certainly not. One or the other, but not both."

"Then why the hell are you destroying her!" he roared.

Jeremiah lifted an eyebrow, a slow smile spreading across his face. "Me?" He let out a wheeze of a laugh. "Did you ever wonder why I tried to kill her in the first place? For such a fierce man, you are quite dumb, Gabriel. Unfortunately, I am running thin on time, and so is our dear Charlotte. I would find her quick before Barbara does. I have a bit of preparation to do—"

With a snarl and a bone breaking lunge, Gabe was thrust from his immobile prison and was moving through the shadows, his fingers breaking and lengthening and claws glinting in the moonlight before he even reached Jeremiah.

Jeremiah was immobile, so deathly calm that Gabe didn't see his hand rise until he felt the feather light touch on his chest. A shock jolted him straight, eyes wide and dazed, as the symbol on the old man's hand rested close to Gabe's heart.

"You have a warrior's soul," Jeremiah said seriously, respectfully, "and a foolish heart."

Jolts of visions stole the breath from Gabe's lungs and took him to a place far, far away from this dark, dismal forest. "You are worthy to be a king, Gabriel, and be trusted as a mate. Find Charlotte. Hold her for a while longer." His old hand pressed harder into Gabe's chest and made the beast's heart slam within the confines of his body, his wide blue eyes water, his mouth agape, and his eyes stare into nothing yet see everything all the same.

"I'm giving you this, these visions, this future," Jeremiah muttered, losing his own breath as he lost his strength. He gave Gabe a future with Charlotte, a future where she wasn't cursed to die, where her mind wasn't lost, where she was wholly and completely Charlotte and nothing else. "Hold onto these when she's gone. Hold onto this future until you can create a better one."

And when Gabe blinked his eyes, mouth opening and closing with soundless words, Jeremiah was gone. Not even his scent lingered, but the visions he had were seared into Gabe's mind and made his chest ache unbearably. It was only a moment longer before he took off into the woods himself.

If it had been Jeremiah's intention to force Gabe into a decision of saving his mate or his pack, then the old man was a fool.

Jeremiah had given Gabe those visions as an impossible future to hold onto when Charlotte was gone, a parting gift to always wonder what it really would have been like if Charlotte lived. But Gabe would do anything to make that impossible future real, to always have her by his side with their pack alive and well before them.

Gabe was allowed his own moments of madness too.

Out there in the woods, Charlotte felt incredibly and wholly alone. The trees, the shadows, the tiny sounds the night made while it slept reminded her there was plenty around her to give her company, yet for some reason, it did nothing to comfort her.

Especially not when she couldn't remember how she had gotten out here or where exactly 'here' was.

The cold hit her like a slap, and Charlotte flinched from it, her hair whipping about her. Oh no, oh no, oh no. Not again. She had lost a moment, a whole entire day, and had no recollection of it at all. Worse yet, she had no idea where the bloody hell she was. She let out a frantic sob and held her hands up to either side of her head, squeezing her eyes shut and holding onto her temples like she could stop her brutalized mind from escaping any further. With a gasp from a throbbing, sharp pain, she pulled her left hand forwards to see three knuckles shattered, swollen, and stiff from the cold.

"Please," she said softly. "Please, please." But she wasn't sure what she was begging for anymore. The strength left her, and she fell to her knees. She felt sane, if only for a moment, but how sane was she anymore? She was in the forest in the long shirt and shorts she had been in hours earlier surrounded by a circle of runes. She couldn't feel her fingertips nor remember leaving her grandmother's house. Had she broken a rune? It certainly would explain her shattered hand, but not where the hell her grandma had been when she did escape.

Hot tears of exhaustion stung her eyes. She gripped the dirt of the forest floor and let her fingertips dig into the soil in a desperate ploy to ground herself in any way. Her grandma was trying to kill her. Her grandpa was trying to kill her. Gabe had abandoned her, and she was losing her mind.

"Please." She begged and sobbed into the shadows of the forest.

"Helium." She hiccupped. "Neon, Radium, Krypton, Xenon." She closed her eyes tight and pictured the noble gasses on the periodic table. She needed her mind, needed her own thoughts, needed something sane. She was alone out there. Her mind was going, her sanity was fading, and she was alone.

Her good hand dug at the ground a little deeper, absentmindedly drawing symbols with her fingertips. The dirt piled beneath her fingernails and stained her knees while she knelt there. She turned as she drew, blinking away her teary eyes and hiccupping as she spoke quietly to herself. "Lithium, Sodium, Potassium," she said more sternly, with more conviction. She turned on her knees in a small circle, drawing and surrounding herself tightly with beautiful artwork... with poetry only the elders would be able to read and only Charlotte could understand. "Rubidium, Cesium."

When she was done, she sat back on her heels and wiped her face with her dirt covered fingers, smearing mud on her tear-stained cheeks. She let out a long sigh and sat back so she could pull her knees up in front of her and hug them close to her chest. It made her feel surrounded and not so desperately alone.

"I can stay here," she told herself. "I can stay here." In her circle of runes, she was protected. Not against much for Charlotte wasn't nearly as strong as she used to be, but it would be enough for just a little while. When her mind slipped again, it would be enough to keep her out here, away from her grandmother. If her grandpa found her, it would be enough to make him think for a moment of which rune to use to get past her. And if Gabe found her, well, nothing could keep him away. Not that she would ever want to.

She had no strength to try to even remember how she had gotten away from her grandma, or any of the other elders for that matter. In the days her grandma had her, everyone from the council had dropped by to help move Charlotte's demise along faster. It was devastating seeing just how many people were pining for her death, and even more painful to forget for just a second every time her mind went blank, only to wake up and have to remember all over again.

"You're okay, Charlotte," she told herself, leaning forward to rest her forehead against her knees. "Everything's okay."

And from the woods, from the blackened, charred shadows, came a voice stained with the bitter edges of insanity.

With her head lowered and her mind scattered and beaten, Charlotte could hear the rustling of leaves and the sound of twigs snapping as dozens of newcomers decided to drop by to witness Charlotte's last moments of self-sustainability.

"Hey there, girly," the voice greeted, and from the shadows, a maniacal grin stretched across a frantically mad face.

Chapter 25

It was a symphony of snarls, of mad beasts so far outside of their own minds, they didn't feel the pain of the runes surrounding Charlotte until they broke their bones trying to breach it. It was a collage of flashing eyes, shining with the glow of something else, something more, something not... right. It was an image of a girl hugging her knees to her chest, face buried down, surrounded by dozens of beasts spitting and snarling and pushing against her circle of runes.

It was hell, and Charlotte was sure she made it.

"I can think." Came a gnarled voice from the darkness, rising among the snarls of his companions. "I can think clearly for the first time. These symbols on me, on us, it takes our madness and it... it sets us free."

As the beasts moved and clawed at the runes, she could feel them within her, the energy the symbols were pulling. She could feel it thinning. She was losing her own mind, losing her will to place power behind her own protection.

"It's been so, so long since I could think," he said, his voice carrying its own entity like it could break through Charlotte's rune boundary and strangle her, "since I could put a reason to things. All it took was a small symbol. It didn't even hurt."

"And now you're someone's bitch for the rest of your life," Charlotte mumbled into her knees. She was so exhausted, so tired, she couldn't even feel afraid of the monsters pawing at her. She just felt a delirium pushing her towards an imminent edge, and it made her laugh to herself as she huddled on the dirt. "That's so much better, Cepheus. You've finally got that free will you always wanted to be able to never do anything for yourself. Was it my grandma, or my granddad?" She didn't even know who was trying to kill her anymore.

"Barbara." He sniffed. A chill wafted through the darkness and bit into Charlotte's skin. "She's a very kind woman."

"Her only flaw was the murder of her granddaughter. I can see how that's easy to overlook." She lifted her head, eyes glinting just as mad as the beasts around her, and instantly caught the eyes of the only man in the clearing. "This isn't freedom, Cepheus. It's changing out the chains in your mind for the chains of the elders."

She couldn't see him, not with the darkness as prominent as it was, but his eyes caught the moonlight and flashed with fury, jolting her deep in her chest. For a quick moment, shorter than the length of a heartbeat, Charlotte came back into her own mind and was paralyzed with intense fear at the scene before her... of the claws and teeth gnashing inches from her, of the matted fur and spittle, of the smell of rot, and of the overwhelming ache to find Gabe.

Then she was gone just as quick, numb and cold once more.

"When she has you, I'll have the pack." Cepheus declared. "I want you to know that as you're dying, I'll be killing your beast."

A slow, wretchedly beautiful smile spread across Charlotte's face. It was so serene, so peaceful, that the snarling beasts around her took pause to stare at the fire-haired girl before them.

"He's the king of beasts." She noted quietly. "There is no killing him."

The next hit to her cocoon of safety sent a tremor deep into her chest, knocking the breath from her lungs, as a set of teeth sunk deep, deep into her ankle.

The blood, the stench, the feel, and the knowledge that it was Charlotte's…

Hurt, she was hurt. Charlotte was hurt and bleeding a lot. It was not enough to kill, but enough to hurt. *Blood.* Charlotte was bleeding.

Moving fast, but not fast enough… faster, faster, *faster…*

Trees, darkness, and the breeze was running with him, on his side, on his team, pushing him towards Charlotte.

The sound of snarling beasts, the stench of rotting decay, and the last threads of humanity in Gabe's mind fled the moment he made it to her.

It was just the beast, just the monster, bearing down on a group of mad animals with his mate, his soul, his life, held in their jaws.

There was no stopping him now.

There was never any hope, ever, to stop the king of beasts.

When the first beast died at the jaws of the king, a massive tremor shot through the boundary line. It was an earthquake only those capable could feel. It rose up from the ground, sending jolts of electricity to their fingertips.

The fault line was breaking, shattering. Just a breeze now, a sneeze in the wrong direction, would shatter the entire thing, taking away with it centuries worth of growth, strength, and life.

And one way or another, it would all end on this night.

It could be from Barbara, hobbling through the woods towards where she knew her beasts were with an unfamiliar desperation clawing apart her insides.

Or maybe Jerimiah would finish it although he was far away… an entire state away. He was in a hospital room, standing beside the bed of a girl with hair so black, it caught the light and almost seemed purple. There was a tube down her throat forcing air into lungs that couldn't work anymore on their own, making the body live while the mind had left a long, long time ago. It was a shell, a perfect, perfect shell, one of which Jerimiah etched a tiny symbol on right behind the left ear. If you looked fast enough, it almost seemed like a flower, circling and looping and utterly beautiful in its own right.

And maybe it would be Charlotte who would finish it off... finish herself off. Maybe her own mind would split in half, and she would give the elders just what they needed: a kick in the ass to get out of there and find another fault line to live on.

One way or another, it would end soon, and it would end on this very night.

And oh, how incredible it was going to be.

Chapter 26

They were everywhere, biting into his hind legs, clawing at his shoulder, and one going for his jugular. The smell was overwhelming and nearly made him delirious, almost making him just as mad as the beasts he was fighting.

Fur was clenched in his jaws, and his sharp eyes were sharper than ever. He was completely and utterly the beast. Nothing more, nothing less. Instinct ruled every motion, every thought, so that the only thing that made sense was that his mate was getting dragged across the clearing by a set of sharp jagged teeth, and he was going to kill the beast doing it to her.

Pain wasn't a factor. Not now. Later? Yes, he would definitely feel it later, every bite, scratch, and broken bone healing itself back together. But now, pain was a hindrance, and the beast had no time for any hindrances. When he was brought down to the ground, for just a moment, of course, it was from the lack of strength in his back leg where a gnarled looking rogue had bitten into his leg.

One grabbed onto his shoulder, trying to bring him down completely, but the fool was dead in the next moment. He was stupid for trying to take his mate, and stupider for trying to kill the king. Just plain stupid.

Bodies piled around him like a morbid meadow, a savage display of the evidence towards the mighty power held within the king of beasts.

Unfortunately, though, reality will show that no matter the strength, one beast will find it near impossible to take down dozens of others on his own.

He couldn't shake the rogue on his back leg and couldn't dodge the rogue leaping through the air, knocking him on the side. He stumbled and caught his footing but refused to fall—then claws swiped his side and blood fell in the aftermath, and he was falling to the side anyways, unable to stop it.

He caught sight of Charlotte while he laid on his side. He saw her move her free leg back and smash it right onto the forehead of the beast holding her. He heard the yelp. He would have grinned. He would have gone over there, picked her up, and kissed her right then if he wasn't bleeding out onto the forest floor with what seemed like a sea of rogues threatening to tear him apart.

She caught his eye, though, and he saw how very little was left of his Charlotte. How mad those green eyes were. She saw him, though. Charlotte saw Gabe, and for a brief moment those green eyes lit up brilliantly, and she was screaming his name, screaming for him, as she clambered over tree roots. "Gabe!" she cried. "*Gabriel!*"

He swiped at a rogue going for his throat, struggled to his feet, and felt teeth sink into the back of his neck and drag him back down.

"GABE!" Her voice was wretchedly horrified and scared. The king of beasts was snarling, drowning in the river of growls and swiping claws around him. There were teeth in his flank and another swipe at his already injured side. He was going down. He had killed thirteen beasts in two minutes and forty seconds, and the other dozen or so were about to kill him quite brutally, in half that time.

Then they would take Charlotte. Then they would kill her too.

He saw red. He saw her hair reflecting the moonlight, and he let it burn like a furious fire behind his eyes. Red. Blood, Charlotte's hair, and the rising sun she always adored watching. It was red like burning embers scorching his skin and turning his mind blank.

The beast at his hind leg was swept away suddenly, and the pressure of teeth leaving was followed by a pathetic whimper. Recognition carried on the wind as a howl sounded as four more growls filled the clearing, and the beast biting his flank was ripped away the same time the one on his back was.

Odin had arrived, and he had brought the three wolves Gabe had demanded to follow him in search for Jason.

The rest was easy. It was not even a competition.

The rogues suddenly seemed scarcer. Those capable ran into the shadows while those not died right then. It was finished quickly, leaving a graveyard in its wake. The king of beasts struggled to his feet on shaking legs. No weight could be placed on his back leg, and it felt like if he sneezed, his kidney might just fall out of his side, but he was on his feet, and he was stumbling towards Charlotte.

"You came." She gasped, sobbing and moving to her own feet. She sagged against a tree, losing strength in her body and her injured left foot. "I didn't think... I thought you were gone. Gabe, god, stop moving. You're going to kill yourself."

Stop moving? Stop moving towards her, leaning against that oak and bleeding? Stop advancing towards the most beautiful thing he had ever seen even with her skin covered in grime and blood, her shirt ripped, and her hair a burning mess?

He would never stop moving towards her. He would never let her get away.

He shifted in a haze of brutal agony a few steps from her, and when he was on his feet, injuries painfully made themselves aware on his naked skin. He grabbed Charlotte and tugged her against his chest before she could protest. A hand tangled in her hair, and the other wrapped around her shoulders. He panted, exhausted and in pain, but the feeling of her against him rivaled all else.

She was perfection, and she was in his arms once more.

"I'm so sorry." He breathed heavily against the top of her head. Her hands splayed over his chest, fingers curling in on themselves. "I'm so sorry, Charlotte."

"It's okay." She nodded her head against him, and he felt hot tears scorch his chest. "You're here. I-I feel sane. I can think. I haven't been able to for days. I thought you weren't coming."

He clenched his eyes shut, a different pain decimating the space in his chest. "I'll always come for you, Charlotte. I promise, always."

"I know." She placed a soft, delicate kiss on the center of his chest and lifted her head so their eyes could meet. Her hand splayed over the space she had just touched her lips to, and she nodded her head as if affirming something to herself. "It's you and me, right? Me and you. We can take on the world. I know it."

He smiled, a smile so brilliant, it hurt her eyes to stare at him. He was perfect.

He held onto her the next second when her eyes flashed, and she didn't recognize the man before her. When she found herself in the arms of a stranger, all she could do was scream, and scream, and scream, and no matter how much she hit against his chest and threatened the man for her release, he held on tight.

But she had said it was Charlotte and Gabe against the world, and he would make sure he never let her go and that she'll be around to face this brutally messed up world with him.

Chapter 27

"Look at me." It was a soft demand, just brushing past the boundaries of her mad, mad mind. "Look at me. Come on, just look at me, Charlotte."

It was dark in her mind, dark, shadowed, and confusing. It seemed like there was nothing there, yet she could feel it, feel the madness and her every thought and memory pressing down on her, and pushing, pushing, pushing until it seemed like she was about to be crushed.

It was very dark in her mind indeed.

"Charlotte, look at me!" It was a desperate plea now, sharper than before. It was a velvet voice wafting through this murky river Charlotte floated upon, caressing her body and making her want, for just a second, to stop drifting upon the endless sea of her mind. But what else was there besides this darkness?

"Come back to me, baby. Come back. Look at me!" She jolted as she felt the words like raw power, but a dark mind has a dark strength, and it sucked Charlotte deeper down the current of her insanity.

Not yet, Charlotte, a new voice whispered. This one was different yet familiar, like it was in her mind with her, beside her on this dark river. *Hold out a bit longer, baby girl. You can do it. You're strong, Charlie. Show them all how strong you are.*

It was her grandpa. The memory of him, his smile, the laughter lines around his never-aging face, his tuft of hair atop his head, and the freckle on the tips of his nose burst through the darkness and pierced Charlotte.

The darkness carried on its own down the river, but Charlotte, grounded once more, stayed behind. She blinked her eyes open and saw a face, a beautiful, beautiful face staring at her with a canopy of trees and a few twinkling stars behind him.

"Hey," he said, fingers running over her face, down her cheek, and across her jaw like he was trying to keep her grounded. "Hey, Charlotte. That's it. That's it, baby, stay right here. Stay here with me, alright?"

"Gabe." She sighed, feeling the moss and leaves against her back and a tree root digging into her shoulder. Her ankle seared with pain, and her hand was throbbing to her heartbeat. He was covered in dirt and blood, yet she saw no wounds on him, just shallow cuts that were healing even as she watched. "Oh, Gabe." Too many things were resting right at the tip of her tongue, and they were too many to say, about how much she loved him and how it was so consuming, it nearly hurt… how she felt as though he had taken a piece of her soul all for himself, and she couldn't imagine anything better than that. But the words caught in her throat. There were too many things to say, and yet there was no way to make them sound important.

He nodded his head, dipping low to press his face into the crook of her neck. He inhaled deeply, his body shuddering. "I know, I know." His hand smoothed down the tangled greasy mess that was her hair. He pulled back, his lips centimeters above her own, so they were breathing the same cool night air. "I feel it too."

He kissed her slow and sweet, and she could feel it, he could feel it, they both felt it. This was a different power. This was a different energy. His lips were hot on hers, and her lips were cool on his. There was no hope, really, not for either of them, but if this was as close as their souls could ever feel, if this moment was the moment they would remember until everything else ended, it would be good enough. It would always be good enough.

"You can't leave me," Gabe said softly against her lips so his breath fanned her cheeks. "You can't, Charlotte. You can't leave me behind."

She closed her eyes tight and shuddered in his hold. "Never," she forced herself to say. "I'll never leave you." A hand pressed against his chest so she could feel his beating heart beneath her palm.

She stared up at him, and he stared down at her. They both knew neither had a choice. Charlotte would go, and she would leave Gabe behind.

"You're the king of beasts," she said into the thin night air. "Nothing can take you down. Please don't let me be the first to do so."

He shook his head, the sharp stubble along his jaw tickling Charlotte's hand when she pressed it to the side of his face. "You will always be the only person to bring me to my knees." He turned his head and pressed his lips to her hand.

"The others?" she asked, clearing her throat and referring to the others beasts who had been in the clearing the last she remembered. Odin had been here with some others, but their part of the forest was empty now.

"Chased after the last of the rogues and went to get more help."

She nodded, closing her eyes again. In the back of her head, she could feel the darkness running down that river trying to pull her back in.

It's time for us to talk now, sweetheart.

Her eyes snapped open and stared hard into the blue depths of Gabe's eyes, seeing the confusion on his face at her sudden anxiety.

"Charlotte?" He shifted and leaned closer. "What's wrong?"

What was wrong was that she could see the stars at the tree tops beyond his shoulder, and she could see a man stepping from the shadows, leaning down, and silently placing a hand on Gabe's arm.

She felt him go rigid and suck in a sharp breath. She saw him widen his eyes down at her before tumbling away. He fell in a heap on his side, breathing heavy with his eyes open and moving about like he was watching a movie.

Charlotte shouted, scrambling to her senses. She reached for Gabe, but he didn't move. He was alive and breathing but frozen.

"He's fine." Her grandad assured her. "He's someplace else, dreaming of something better than this."

She looked up into the sea-green eyes of who had been her closest friend. "What did you do?" she cried, trying to bring herself to her feet to inflict some sort of harm upon the monster before her.

"He's in his own head, Charlotte, living in a future I gave to him. He'll come back, I promise you that. I need to speak with you honey, and he'll get in the way."

"There's nothing you can say that I want to hear," she spat at him, finding she couldn't stand or defend herself. So instead, she turned over and curled into Gabe's side, deciding maybe she could protect him with what little life she had left. It wouldn't do much, if anything, but she would do it anyways.

"He's not going to make the choice, Charlie," he told her quietly. "He can't."

Her eyes flickered up to her grandpa. He looked so much older now under the moonlight. "What choice?" she asked.

"You, or the pack."

"Me or the—What the hell are you talking about?"

"If you live on without completing the bond, you'll destroy the pack. If you die, they move on."

She looked back at Gabe with widened eyes, then they narrowed. Her grandad was a snake, a cruel man, and his words felt like lies to her. He was here to kill her, finally, and he was making it as torturous as he could.

"You, though, Charlie, I think you can make the choice."

"I have a choice?" she asked sarcastically. "Is it to die here, or die someplace else?"

He was silent, and she looked up to see a deep aching sadness turn his eyes a dark green. "A choice to die by your grandmother or to die by me."

She closed her eyes tight, her chest aching right under her scar. "I don't understand," she whispered, pulling herself closer to Gabe's side. "I don't get why you're both so desperate to kill me. You're serving the same cause, why do it separately? Why did she lock you up if you were just doing what they wanted?"

She didn't know he had moved until she felt his hand on her shoulder. She jerked away, and he pulled back. She kept her eyes shut tight, feeling Gabe's body heat against her.

"I was a fool to take part in the council for so long," he muttered quietly. "A mad fool. When you were born, I knew it was too late to take back what we had already started, and that will always be my gravest mistake. You were destined to die from your very first breath."

She heard him shift and sigh deeply.

"If you die by the hands of you grandmother, she's taking every life within the town alongside you. Every soul, every scrap of energy, will be taken. The boundary around the town will fall away, outsiders will wander in, and they will find a town filled with hundreds of bodies staring at nothing." There was another pause. "And a few miles away, a town filled with beasts staring into that same nothingness."

Her chest squeezed, strangling her with pain. "And you agreed to this?" she whispered. "You agreed to kill all these people?"

"Yes." There was no hesitation. He wasn't about to deny his acts, not now. "I agreed, and then I didn't."

She took a long moment to feel Gabe beside her before turning her head to see her granddad crouching a foot away from her. "You tried to kill me."

"Yes, I did." He nodded his head. "I tried to kill you very normally, very brutally… no circle of runes and no flashy wards. I tried to kill you so normally that there was no grounding of your soul or the profuse amount of energy stored within. I tried to kill you so that the power released would have shattered the fault line right then, right at that moment, and it all would have been over. We would have died and drifted away very quietly into the night."

She blinked slowly, unsure if there was any right way to process this. "My soul's locked now," she said quietly. "That's why you had those beasts attack me."

He shook his head once. "That wasn't me. That was your fabulous, theatrical grandmother." He closed his eyes and pinched the bridge of his nose. "The council was ready to destroy hundreds of lives to live longer than anyone should. I thought I could do that too, but it turns out I couldn't. I'm only sorry I didn't realize that before you were born."

Charlotte closed her eyes tightly, feeling the dark river of her mind pulling her down again. "How can my grandma killing me be any different than you doing it? How can it save anything?"

"You need a very specific place and a very specific set of runes to harvest the pieces of your soul that are storing the chips from the fault line. They would harvest it and use it to harvest the souls in this town and carry on their merry way."

Charlotte blinked once. "Excuse me? I have chips of the fault line in my soul?"

Her grandpa sighed. "I've found a way to make this right, Charlie. I had it prepared when you were nine years old, but your grandmother got there before it was finished. I've finally got it together once more. Hate me. I deserve it. I need you to hate me, but I know you can't sacrifice two towns. I know you, Charlie. Let me explain."

She looked back at Gabe, her eyes draping over the line of his jaw and her fingers following its path. She had no strength and no hope. Her granddad could kill her right then, and she would be powerless to stop him, yet he stood there quietly waiting for her to make a choice. A choice of her death, but a choice nonetheless.

She leaned down and pressed her lips gently to his, breathing him in and savoring him, before pulling back. "He'll come back?" she asked, motioning to Gabe's wide, dazed eyes.

Jeremiah nodded. "He'll be fine. You have my word."

"Your word means nothing to me," she said flatly, but no matter how dull she sounded, the words had enough bite in them to make him flinch. "But if I had a choice, a choice at all, I'd like to hear why and how this all happened and what your plan is."

Jeremiah nodded, eyes serious and dark, and held out his hand. Charlotte was done pausing, done waiting, and grabbed onto it so he could haul her to her feet. "I still have time to make up for my mistakes, Charlie. Just you wait."

She certainly didn't have much time either way.

Chapter 28

The sun was warm, and the breeze was cool. A cloud strolled on by above as an ant made the treacherous journey across the ground below. Gabe stood back, blinking slowly. He could see the roof of his house just ahead and the forest to his back. How had he gotten here? He couldn't remember where he had been in the first place.

Meanwhile, red hair swayed in the breeze and caught the sunlight. A breath was caught in his throat as he stared at the scene of swaying grasses and the sound of feminine laughter. His chest ached in the best of ways when a pair of green eyes turned and met his... when Charlotte paused her chase and gave him a wave.

And the little girl by her side stumbled suddenly, tripping over her little feet, and she and her own red hair went tumbling to the ground.

Charlotte turned and bent down, gently plucking the little girl to her feet, and another round of laughter ensued as they dusted themselves off.

Rosie. Her name was Rosie.

He stared at her, and his own eyes stared back at him as she waved enthusiastically. She had Charlotte's hair and his eyes, and when she ran across the backyard to him, he crouched low to scoop her up in his arms.

"That was quite the fall." He chuckled as she spun around in his hold, lifting a knee to show the small cut adorning it.

"Yea, I got a cut," she said, eyes wide with excitement. "It's even bleeding, Dad!"

Charlotte strolled up to them, tucking her head into Rosie's neck and blowing until the girl was squealing and nearly tumbled out of his arms. Gabe lowered her to the ground, and she took off the next second, hunting down the ground that dared to harm her.

Charlotte watched her go and turned to Gabe with a roll of her eyes. "I swear, she's going to jump off a roof one of these days to see if she can fly."

"She probably could." Gabe shrugged, watching Charlotte as she watched their daughter. "She can do anything."

Charlotte laughed and turned to glance up at him. She and Rosie shared the same sound. Her eyes sparkled as the sunlight kissed her cheeks. He loved her, loved every bit of her, loved her in the sunlight, in the rain, in the dark. He grinned down at her, and quite suddenly, bent to scoop her into his arms and over his shoulder.

"Gabriel!" she shrieked, grabbing onto his back and shoulder for balance. "What in the holy hell are you doing!"

He grabbed onto the back of her legs, securing her as he strolled across the lawn. "There's storm clouds coming in. I don't want to be out here when it rains."

She spluttered and shrieked when it felt like she was going to fall. Not like Gabe would ever let her fall. "You know, Gabe, there's this funny thing called walking."

He let out a laugh and stopped beside Rosie with his hand held out to hers as she crouched to the ground and plucked a piece of grass. "Mom! Mom, I think it's doing that photo thing! I think it's taking those pictures!"

She looked up and blinked at Gabe and Charlotte. "Daddy, what are you doing with Mom?"

"We're going inside, sweetheart. I think it's going to rain."

She blinked again then stood up, dusting her hands off the side of her shirt. "Oh." She lifted her arms up, blinking those bright blue eyes at him. "I don't want to walk back either."

Charlotte laughed on his shoulder, blood rushing to her head, and Gabe's heart swelled as he picked his little girl up and sat her right on his other shoulder. Her small hands grasped at his head, pulling his hair painfully, and her heels hit his chest. His neighbor, Sam, and his mate, Sydney, glanced up from their back porch, titled their head to the side, and offered a wave at the sight of their queen hauled over their king's shoulder.

They gave a synchronized wave back though Charlotte was upside down and Rosie was sitting on his shoulder, and

Gabe greeted back with a tilt of his head seeing as his hands were occupied.

"You're so going to pay for this." Charlotte giggled from her spot, and Gabe grinned, knowing he certainly would, and he couldn't wait.

He blinked, staring at the fire in the hearth and feeling the warmth lick his skin. It was dark outside, and the only light was the orange glow from the burning logs. The couch was soft against his back, and when he looked down, he saw Charlotte and her red hair splayed out. He tried for a brief moment remembering how they got here, what time had transpired, but the thoughts drifted away as quickly as they came.

She had a book in her hands, eyes scanning the pages as her head rested in his lap. Her feet hung over the edge of the couch, kicking at the air restlessly. His fingers were combing through her hair, feeling how soft and fiery it was.

She felt his gaze, looked up to see him staring, and rolled her eyes. "What did I tell you about the staring, Gabe?"

He grinned, and she went back to her book. His free hand rested on her stomach, so large now, she could rest her book against it as a stand. It was bigger than she ever was with Rosie. Not that he would ever, ever tell her that. He felt a kick under his palm, his grin deepening. "Gabe, the staring," Charlotte commented without looking up, then her own grin tugged at her lips.

"Rosie's still pissed about the whole sibling thing. We should have had another one when she was still young and didn't understand what a brother was," she commented, dog-earing her book and closing it. She sighed, shifted her position with a wince to her aching back, and stared up at Gabe.

"You shouldn't swear. The baby can hear it," he mumbled, rubbing a hand over her stomach.

"Gabe, don't tell an eight-month-old pregnant woman what to say," she snapped without any real bite to her voice, closing her eyes sleepily.

"Of course not." He agreed. He closed his own eyes, running his fingers through her hair. "Maybe we'll have a Christmas baby."

"I certainly hope not," she quipped easily. "A kid likes having his birthday and his Christmas presents separate."

"How would you know?"

She shrugged. "I wouldn't want it."

He had to agree. "Baby Michael." He sighed, rubbing his hand over her stomach and feeling another kick. "Maybe he'll have your eyes."

"No way. He's gotta have yours. He'll be a lady killer for sure."

"What does it make Rosie then?"

"A heartbreaker."

He threw his head back and laughed, fighting the urge to growl in rage at the thought of a boy coming near his little girl, and Charlotte chuckled beneath him, placing her hand on top of his. "You're happy, right?" she asked suddenly. Gabe opened his eyes to see her looking up at him.

Was Charlotte being insecure? Charlotte was never insecure. She wore her frizzy hair down and clothes with paint on them, and she walked around with confidence because she knew she was beautiful. She knew she was perfect as she was.

But she looked up at him now, and he could see the questions burning her eyes.

"Of course, I am," he mumbled, bending down to steal a kiss. "I'm happy. I'm fulfilled. I'm in love with you, my daughter, and my son. I'm happy, Charlotte. I'm always happy with you."

She grinned and pulled him down for another kiss. "If I wasn't so pregnant, I'd climb you like a tree."

He laughed again, feeling a nudge at the back of his head that something, somehow, wasn't right... but it was gone the next second as Charlotte fell asleep against him and he enjoyed this small, significant moment quietly.

He turned the phone off, stopping himself just barely from slamming it against the counter. He had done that to one too many phones, and Charlotte got more and more pissed each time he did it.

He ran a hand through his hair and blinked stupidly as he stood in his kitchen. How had he gotten here?

His anger momentarily forgotten, he turned slowly. His head ached. He had been on the couch with Charlotte just a moment ago, hadn't he? But no, he could remember faintly, like *a ghost print, that years had passed... endless hours. What was wrong with him?*

"What was that about?"

His head turned to the doorway where Charlotte leaned. She wore an old gray sweatshirt, a pair of worn jeans, and specks of paint in her red hair. She had come from her workspace, and he could smell the fumes of her art from across the room.

His confusion forgotten and his anger remembered, he let out a huff. "The land was breached again. I have to promote most of my trainees now to get more warriors. At this rate, I'm going to turn my entire town into an army."

He ran his hand through his hair once more, closing his eyes and leaning against the countertop behind him. God, his head was hurting. How had he gotten here again?

When he felt Charlotte's hands against his chest, every muscle sagged in relief like they had been crying out for her this entire time. "You're a good man, you know that?" she asked quietly.

He peeked an eye open to glance down at her, paint soaked and grinning with that peculiar sparkle in her green eyes. Michael got her eyes this time, much to her despair, and her nose. He had also grown so fast. Rosie had grown even faster, and now, his little girl was putting eyeliner on, and her shorts kept getting shorter. The boys kept coming to his house, and he didn't know how many more he could scare away.

Charlotte's hands rubbed at his chest, bringing him back and relaxing him. "You think so?" he mumbled, a grin tugging up the corner of his mouth.

She hummed, leaning in closer. "I'm pretty certain I wouldn't stick around with a bum."

"So if I was a bum, you'd ditch me?"

"In a heartbeat," she grinned, and he laughed, and she leaned up on her toes to press a soft kiss to his jawline. God, she was incredible.

"You know you still have an hour before your meeting," she mumbled.

"Do I?" he asked quietly, his hands running up her sides and dipping under that god awful sweatshirt that hid every bit of her.

"Mhmm." Her lips glided across his neck, kissing the spot under his ear. A rumble built in his chest. "And the kids are at school for even longer."

"Are they?"

Her fingers tugged at the hem of his shirt. Her palms were placed against his abdomen, rubbing at his skin and back over his chest. "Mhmm." Her tongue darted out, tasting the column of his neck, and he shuddered. A big man like Gabe was crumbling at the feet of his mate.

"What do you suppose we do with so much free time?" He grinned, wrapping his arms around her waist, tugging her even closer, and breathing in that delicious, dizzying smell so the ache in his head began fading back into nothing.

"Remember after that cook out Odin had?" she asked, and oh yes, he remembered that well. "Because I can remember it." She tugged his shirt up, he lifted his arms to help remove it, and she tossed it aside. She placed a soft, delicate kiss on the center of his chest, her eyes flickering up to meet his. *"I remember how I thought the counter couldn't possibly be a good place for you to blow my mind."*

She patted the said granite block behind Gabe, a grin tugging up her lips. Gabe growled low in his throat and grabbed her hips to lift her up and around so she was sitting on the counter. She squealed, grabbing onto his shoulders before laughing.

"I remember proving you wrong if that's what you mean," he said, moving to stand between her legs, to cup her face in both of his hands and bring her close. He paused, lips centimeters from hers. That same thought, asking him what was happening, was nagging at the back of his head. How had he gotten here? What had happened in the last years? Why did his head hurt?

But Charlotte leaned in, closing the distance, and the feel of her lips on his erased all other thoughts.

It was her and him, alone in their kitchen with articles of clothing slipping away, that terrible sweatshirt finally leaving her skin. Her jeans came next, tugged so fast from her that she jumped and burst into a fit of giggles that Gabe turned into a soft sigh with a kiss to her stomach. His fingers brushed over the stretch mark lining her side, reminding him of the extraordinary gifts she had given him.

Leaning back, she ran her hands through his hair, drawing his gaze up to her, and the power behind those green eyes struck him speechless. At this moment, at this second, she could steal his beating heart right from his chest, and he would allow it. At this moment, at this second, there was Charlotte, there was Gabe, and there was the thrumming of their souls intertwining with one another.

Their souls—their souls? Why didn't that sound right? No... No, because Charlotte couldn't connect. Charlotte's soul was locked. They couldn't complete the bond. None of this was real.

Her hands ran down his chest and across his abdomen, grabbing onto his belt and flicking it open. "I know, you're a patient man, but I'm not a very patient woman, Gabe," she mumbled, tugging the belt from the loops. He grinned as she deposited the belt beside her on the counter top, their eyes meeting once more.

"Your wish is my command, my lady."

She leaned forwards and wrapped her hands around his neck, nuzzling herself closer. Gabe's fingers brushed up her back, following her spine and massaging the base of her neck. He brushed a bra strap to the side, kissing her exposed shoulder. "I kind of want another one," he mumbled against her skin as his hand brushed across her stomach.

"No way in hell." She sighed, combing his hair with her fingers. "You try shoving a kid out of you twice and then say you want another one."

He laughed, switching sides, brushing her other bra strap away, and running his nose across her shoulder. "You think I can convince you?"

She sagged against his hold, letting out a slow breath. "I would love nothing more than to see you try."

He loved a good challenge.

He kissed the spot where her neck and shoulder met, his hands tracing the path of her bra and reaching for the hook. He kissed her behind her ear, felt her tremble, felt victorious.

And then he stopped. There was a mark on the back of her neck, one that had never been there before. His hands left her bra and brushed her hair to the side, looking at the scar-like mark on the back of her neck. If he looked fast enough, it almost looked like a flower.

A rune.

The words jolted him and had him taking a step back. "Gabe?" Charlotte tilted her head to the side, concerned. "What's wrong?"

Runes... her granddad... Charlotte's soul... runes... She was dying. Charlotte was dying, and none of this, absolutely none of it, was real.

"Oh, Charlotte," he said, hand grasping at his chest where an unbelievable pain blossomed. He stared at his beautiful mate, his future Charlotte with her long red hair and tiny wrinkles around her eyes, evidence of the years spent laughing, his Charlotte who had given him two beautiful children... his Charlotte who loved him right back.

And his Charlotte, who sat there and blinked, cleared her throat. "Look for the rune, alright?" she said.

"The rune?" God, this wasn't real... this wasn't real. It was not real.

"Gabe," she snapped, stopping him, "this is extraordinarily important. Look for the rune, alright?" She brushed her hair to the side and showed the flower rune. "Find this, and you've found me."

"Charlotte, no, don't go. Don't go." He stumbled closer to her, reaching for her atop the counter. He could feel it slipping and feel the ache in his head. This future was going, leaving him behind. His Charlotte, his daughter, and little

Michael... The memories he had weren't real. This happiness wasn't real. Nothing was. "Oh, god."

And just like that, as suddenly as though she were a passing breeze, she was gone. His children were gone. This future was gone.

The cold night air met him when he blinked again, the stars winking above him. He sucked in a deep breath, felt the ache in his chest, and allowed it to take him back to reality.

He knew instantly Charlotte wasn't beside him, that he had been shoved into the future Jeremiah had allowed him to see, and now he was alone once more. What was more cruel, taking Charlotte away from him or allowing Gabe to see just what they could have had?

He sat and stood up, knowing without a doubt that this was the end. One way or another, it was ending, and he felt it right in the pit of his stomach, and it scared him more than anything else in the entire world. It scared him worse now that he had a clear image of a little girl with Charlotte's red hair and a tiny little boy with her eyes. It terrified him more now that he had seen what he was going to have with her if he could just hold on, if she could just hold on, if a miracle were to occur and the impossible happened.

He took off into the night, thinking of children, and his mate, and runes that looked like flowers if you glanced too quick. He could do it. He could save her. His sanity wouldn't allow anything else.

Chapter 29

This is okay, she thought. *This is okay.* Her neck still ached where the rune was carved in, her body felt sore and exhausted, and she just wanted to sleep, but this was fine. She just wanted to close her eyes and drift away, but this was fine.

"Your grandma is coming," Jeremiah announced, glancing into the shadows of the forest. "She brought some more beasts with her."

Charlotte gritted her teeth. Her mind flashed back and forth quickly now like a shutter. On then off, then on again, forgetting everything then remembering it all at once, emotions overwhelming and then non-existent. She was incredibly tired.

"Gabe should be coming soon." She blinked, refocusing herself. "Odin will probably be right behind him. They can help."

Jeremiah glanced to his granddaughter sitting with her back against an incredibly old oak tree. "Can you do this?" he asked, his voice unsure for what felt like the first time in his long, long life.

Charlotte opened her eyes, and the symbol on the back of her neck burned, flaring to life like a reminder. "It's already done."

His tropical ocean eyes flickered back up to the shadows. "You know I've done all I can, right? All I can possibly do to make this right?"

Charlotte closed her eyes and let the chill of the night wash away all her other worries. "I know." She sighed. "Maybe it'll be enough. I don't know. I'm just very tired, and I want it to all be over."

"It will, soon, sweetheart. Just a little longer."

Just a little longer. She could feel her mind slipping away, the last strings of her sanity snapping. Just a little longer, and there would be nothing left, nothing keeping her here, and she would just... drift away. Until the elders latches onto her drifting soul and feed from the pieces of the fault line trapped within.

Just a little longer than that, and the fault line would shatter completely. The elders would pass on, and then just a tad bit longer and Charlotte would, too. Nothing could save her mind, nothing could save her soul. Nothing could save her.

All that she could really do was wait just a little longer.

Gabe knew exactly where she was. He could smell her in the air like a lit up path leading him to Charlotte. He knew there was no hope, yet he ran on anyways because that's what you are supposed to do when you love someone so much, it breaks you down piece by piece. You run to them anyways.

Odin was behind him, catching up quickly, and behind them were dozens of his warriors. They might face the elders, they might face some more ruthless, mad beasts, and they might face magical dancing forest fairies for all they knew. It didn't hurt to have help.

There was a determination linking the group together, a collective cause that pushed their limbs faster and made their beating hearts sync together as one entity towards one goal. It was to save Charlotte, to save their queen, to bring her home and worship her like they needed to do.

No one but Gabe really knew how pointless it all was, but not even he was ready to admit it.

They quickly knew their opponents were a group of savage rogues when a scent of rot was carried on the breeze. There were a lot of them. Maybe as many as before, but probably more. Luckily, Gabe brought more of his own this time, too. He could smell Jeremiah, Charlotte, and Barbara mingled together in the night.

Dashing through the trees, shadows, and darkness, where not even the moon dared to touch them, the beasts flew. Without words, without a signal, they seemed to understand when Gabe flattened his ears back and gritted his sharp, beastly teeth. *Are we ready*? he seemed to ask, a silent voice bristling over his fur.

And just as collectively, as viciously as their king leading them on, the beasts gritted their own teeth and sent a howl up through the canopy of trees, a symphony of noise to alert those beasts and elders within the clearing seconds before they arrived that they were about to be in the battle of their lives, and they were about to lose.

Moments later, they leaped from the trees and clashed head on with the rogues.

Gabe instantly saw Charlotte sitting with her back against an old oak, her hair brushed back behind her shoulders. Jeremiah and Barbara were nowhere to be seen, having melted into the forest some place.

A path was cleared for Gabe, leading him towards Charlotte who hadn't even glanced up at the commotion and just sat with her head lowered. His heart lurched, his mind automatically thinking she died when he knew it wasn't the case. He would feel it if she died, feel it like a piece of his soul was splintering and rotting away, dying alongside with her. She wasn't dead. Not yet.

The rogues snapped and clawed at him, but his own warriors were trained, and trained well. It wasn't even a fight.

Gabe rushed forwards, head bent, and approached Charlotte. She still hadn't looked up, hadn't opened those beautiful eyes. He was right before her now, and he leaned forward, ready to brush his nose along her jaw and jolt her from whatever sleep she was in, but a burn forced him back inches from touching her face. His snout twitched, and stupidly, he tried again.

When the same result met him, he shifted back into his human form and knelt before her. For the first time ever, the hands of the king of beasts shook and trembled as they reached forward to touch her arm, but his palm was met with the same heat and had him retracting. No matter where he went to touch, the same burn met him and forced him to pull away. He couldn't touch her.

"Charlotte," he said, his voice drowned by the sound of snarling around him. It was loud, nearly deafening in this small space. "Charlotte!"

Her eyes cracked open, her head lifting an inch to look at him. She glanced around the clearing, taking in all the beasts, before turning back to Gabe. "Make sure you keep that window above the kitchen sink closed," she said suddenly. "You always leave it open, and the kitchen is freezing in the morning because of it. It drove me mad."

"Charlotte, what are you—"

"And th-the bed. You put the black pillow on top of the blue one, but it'll look better if you do it the other way around it. Looks nicer." She licked her dry lips. "Go to my house. Make sure my dog isn't still pacing the porch. She was such an asshole, but she was a great dog, and she hates thunderstorms, and I don't know how she'll act if I'm not there."

She closed her eyes, tilted her head to the side, and scrunched up her face like she was in pain. She muttered to herself quickly, shook her head, and opened her eyes once more. A different light shone on them, and Gabe watched her with his own wide eyes. "Charlotte—"

"Gabe!" she shouted, a smile breaking across her face. "I haven't seen you since Jeremiah did his crazy frozen future thing on you. That guy's nuts, right?" She snorted and looked around her once more. "What are they all upset about?" she asked, tilting her head towards the beasts mauling one another.

"Charlotte, look at me," Gabe demanded. She did, shocked by the sharpness of his voice. "Look right at me, Charlotte. Look at me. Come on, Charlotte. Come back to me."

She snorted again and rolled those green eyes of hers. "I *am* here, Gabe. God, you sound crazy t—"

"Charlotte!" He snapped, and her eyes shifted instantly, that crazy gleam extinguishing. She blinked furiously and jolted at the sound of the beasts fighting and at the pain on her neck, hand, and ankle.

She swore loudly, a string of profanities that Gabe didn't even yell at her about. "What's happening?" she cried, her wild, frightened eyes turning to Gabe. "What the hell is happening!"

"Your grandmother must have brought more rogues, so I brought more of my warriors," Gabe said quickly. "Charlotte, I can't touch you. You've got to tell me what's happening. It burns when I get close."

The panic in her eyes died down slightly, sadness seeping in. She lifted her hand like she was going to touch him, then dropped it back in her lap once more. "No one can touch me. Not right now," she said. "My grandma is going to try to get to me, but she can't. No one can with this." She lifted up her hand with the broken fingers, revealing a familiar rune to Gabe. "I bet you can remember this one."

And he did. He remembered it on that same hand, when her wrist was broken, when she was sagged against a flipped car, so determined to not be taken by a beast, she was willing to die on a deserted road instead. She was so fiercely adamant on staying with her own goals, her own idea of what was going to happen, and she was willing to defy fate to do so.

"I touched you, though," Gabe said, looking back up at her sharply. "I touched you with—"

He glanced down, saw blood seeping into the soil from her wounded ankle, and bent to reach it. "Gabriel." She sighed. He looked up and blinked quickly. She had never called him that before, and never in a voice that soft. The snarls, howls, and cries all faded away behind him. The night wasn't so dark, and the air wasn't so cool. It was only Charlotte, Gabe, her soft, sad eyes, and the way she was looking at him at this moment.

"You can't." She shook her head slowly, maintaining eye contact. "If you do that, it breaks the rune, and Barbara can get to me. If she does, then both our towns die."

He blinked again and looked down at the blood-stained soil.

"This way, only I die."

He clenched his eyes shut and gritted his teeth. His chest ached.

"Charlotte, I can't... Y-you can't expect me to accept this. I can't let you do this."

"You have to."

He closed his eyes tighter, hoping the burn in them might go away if he did. "It's me or everyone Gabe. There's no choice to it."

"There has to be another way."

"There's not. I'm so sorry, but there's not."

"I'm supposed to let you die? I'm supposed to step back, not touch you, and let you slip away?" He opened his eyes, angry at the world now, angry at his lack of strength to save her.

She shook her head quickly. "No, no it'll be okay, Gabe. The rune—"

She blinked and cut herself off, that same light coming back into her eyes, and she grinned at Gabe. "Gabe! When did you get here?"

"You've got to be *kidding* me!" He roared, ready to bring her back again, to brush away the insanity for a second longer. A hand lashed out and struck him on his cheek with a surpassing force and knocked him to the side in a daze.

Barbara stepped from the shadows, her lip bleeding, and her own eyes vicious and wild. God, she had a brutal right hook. He could feel it drumming painfully against his skull. She reached for Charlotte and cried out, retracting her hand just as fast, when the rune stopped her. "*No!*" she shrieked.

"Grandma?" Charlotte said, grinning up at her. "What are you doing here?"

"Hey, hey, Charlotte, hey." She brushed a frizzy strand of gray hair from her face. Her hands are shaking, and a tight smile was forming on her face. "You think you can take off that rune on your hand for me?"

Charlotte laughed. "Are you kidding me? You're such a psychotic bitch, why would I ever take this off?" Charlotte glanced at Gabe as he scrambled to his feet and hooked her thumb towards Barbara. "Can you believe her?"

Gabe lunged, ready to take her out finally, but Jeremiah came up behind her looking just as beat up as Barbara and stopped him. "It's alright, Gabe. The fault line's going to break any second."

"No!" Barbara shouted. "No, no, *no!*" She whipped her head around wildly, looking from the fighting beasts to her husband to Gabe then finally landing on Charlotte. She lunged at her, trying again to touch her, and screeched in rage each time she was unable to.

Gabe stood back, unsure of what to do. He heard the noise of battle around him die down as the last of the rogues were killed. Jeremiah stepped forwards and placed his hands carefully on her shoulders to pull her back gently.

Barbara, heaving and hysterical, fought him for just a second before she allowed him to pull her back, her muscles sagging. "This isn't happening," she mumbled and shook her head so what was left of her thin gray hair swayed. "This can't be happening."

He turned her so her eyes were torn from Charlotte as she spoke quietly, madly, to herself. "It's over," Jeremiah said gently as though speaking to a child. "It's done, and there's nothing you can do."

For a brief moment, together like that, Jeremiah and Barbara were kids again. They were getting close to maturity, getting close to having to settle on a territory for the rest of their lives. They were young, and in love, and happy, and everything was okay then.

And now, they were here, in the middle of the night surrounded by dead beasts and their dying granddaughter. "We did this to her," Jeremiah said. "We killed her."

Barbara lowered herself slowly, bringing herself down to her knees, and Jeremiah followed as he kept contact. Gabe went to Charlotte's side where her eyes had closed once more, and he sat before her. His beasts, finished with their battle, stopped and watched on in confusion. They were waiting for their king to rescue their queen.

It was all very quiet, and very peaceful, and when the fault line shattered into indiscernible pieces, obliterated completely and wholly and scattered back into the universe, it didn't make a sound. It just drifted away, taking the lives of thirteen elders with it. Those running through their houses dropped to their floors. Those in bed, knowing the inevitable and wanting to go in their sleep, did.

And Jeremiah and Barbara, holding onto one another, fell to their sides. It really was like sleeping... painless, effortless. They died beside one another holding onto guilt for their granddaughter who would soon follow them, and a thankfulness that there even was guilt at all. Then they were gone, still grasped onto each other as though they didn't want to get lost in death, and they didn't feel much of anything at all.

Charlotte took in a deep, shuttering breath, her eyes widening and her fingers trembling. "Oh, wow," she mumbled, looking at Gabe. "Oh, wow."

Gabe acted quick, drawing his own rune on his chest with her blood like all those nights ago, and grabbed onto her the next second.

Her body seemed to gain ten pounds and dropped to the side, and he followed gently. A hand went to the back of her head to lay it softly on the ground so her wide, wondered eyes could flutter upwards. "Oh wow," she repeated.

"Charlotte? Can you hear me? Are you alright?" He cupped her face with his hands and brushed away the stray hairs.

Her eyes moved over to him, and she grinned. "This feels so bizarre," she whispered. Her eyes moved back upwards, finding the few stars through the canopy of trees. "This feels so... *bizarre*."

"Don't think about it," he said, shaking his head. "Don't think about it. Just stay right here with me."

She let out another breath. She lifted a hand, shaking gently, and rested it on her chest. "I can feel it. I thought it'd hurt but... wow."

Gabe closed his eyes for just a second, feeling in his gut that this would be a perfect moment to give up... to sit quietly beside Charlotte and hold her just like he was doing now and just let her drift away.

"Please, Charlotte, please look at me," he begged, refusing to open his eyes. "Just a little while longer. Just give me a little while longer."

He felt her body heat a second before she placed her hand over one of his. He lifted his head and met her somber gaze. "There's not much left," she said, her lips tilting up. "I don't remember much." She sighed and stared back up. "I don't know if I have a family. I don't know why I'm lying on the forest floor. I don't know why I can feel all these injuries on my body, but I feel so... light. I just... I don't know much. I only know my hair's red because I can see tiny strands of it."

She grinned, then turned her head so her chin rested on her shoulder, and stared at Gabe with bright green eyes. "I remember kissing you, though." She grinned. "You're quite good at it."

He felt his lips tugging up and hated his treacherous face. His insides were ripping apart, very brutally and very painfully, but he was *smiling*.

"I remember you held my face like this when you did it." Her other hand came up to grab his free one against her face. "Please kiss me, Gabe. I like the idea of it being the only thing I remember, but I'm afraid I'm just about to forget it."

He nodded his head mechanically. He felt the force of a deep wish to just be ripped from his body, to not have to watch this happen, then the thought of not being here was even more painful. This was Charlotte, this was his soul, this was his life, and she was asking him to kiss her.

He leaned down and brushed his lips quietly across hers, and she closed her eyes and sighed against him. When her hands fell away, he looked to see her staring at him with something akin to wonder in those eyes. "Insanity feels quite nice," she said quietly, so quiet, it could have easily been taken by a breeze, unheard, if Gabe wasn't so close.

"It's alright," he said to himself and to her. "I'm here. You're alright."

She blinked, and he watched her as she started seeing something else, something more than the dark forest she was in. Those green eyes changed, not with that mad glint they had before but with something different. She had the eyes of someone who was seeing something a person sees only once in their life. Something they see once then goes too fast to tell anyone about it.

"Wait," he said, bringing himself to his knees. "Wait, wait, you can hold on longer, Charlotte."

He hovered above her and grabbed ahold of her shoulder to jolt her, to bring her back from that place. "It doesn't even hurt," she mumbled. "It doesn't even hurt."

"No," he demanded. He was Gabriel. He was the king of beasts. Charlotte couldn't just... She couldn't *leave* him. "Stay here, Charlotte. Damn it, stay with me!" She blinked once, took a breath in, and exhaled.

He felt that last breath on his right cheek. He kneeled there, paralyzed, staring at her with wide eyes like he couldn't quite believe what had just happened. She had done this before, he told himself. She had died before, then he sat back, and she just sat up and started screaming like a maniac. She had done this before. She died, right in his arms, much like she was doing now, and she came back.

She wasn't coming back, though. Not this time.

So he shook her once more. "You can't do this," he said in a choked plea, yet her glassy eyes told him she already had. "You can't! You can't. I don't know how, but we had... we had a little girl, Rosie. She had your hair." A palm brushed over hers then pulled a twig from the red tangles and brushed it from her eyes. "And a little boy. Charlotte, baby, please come back. Please, come back."

And there it was, the king of beasts on his knees, his head tucked into the neck of his mate and begging quietly into the night. The beasts watched on, fresh blood from their battle staining their fur. An unbelievable rumble passed through the clearing, and it became its own life force so you could feel the vibrations in the air.

Because on this night, in the cold and dark, Charlotte died. On this night, amidst the aftermath of chaotic beasts fighting, a queen was swept away. And she left nothing but a shattered community of beasts pining to the night for their ruler, and a king hoping if he holds on just a bit tighter that piece of his soul will come back to him.

Tonight, though, she won't. Tonight, she left them all, and although they couldn't see it, her soul was beautiful and light, and still carried dozens of those fault line chips. Cocooned and kept safe within her soul, they were alive and thrumming and driving her soul through the night.

While it carried on, the night was silent and peaceful, and those in bed continued to sleep while those who waited for the beasts to roam heard nothing. Nothing except for the horrendous cry shattering the silent air, echoing across the night, of a man realizing it was over.

And the echoing howl of dozens of beasts drifted across for miles, all feeling the pain and all crying their beastly cries for it.

Because they were the beasts in the shadows of Harvey's Hill's forest, and their king had just lost his queen.

Chapter 30

There was a girl across the state, past the border, lying in a hospital bed. Her brother had just finished brushing her hair back, and it fell across the white pillow case like spilled ink. He leaned in close, just a few years older than her, and kissed her softly on her forehead with a promise to see her tomorrow.

Alone now, her chest rose on the machine's command and lowered right afterward. There was nothing in that pretty head of hers, no thoughts, no emotions. No soul called her home. No natural life fueled her body. Jane was an empty girl who should have been gone a long, long time ago but who also had an older brother that had just lost both his parents. He couldn't lose his little sister, too, not when their little brother kept asking about her.

It was better to hope for her to breathe on her own when there was no possibility than to pull the plug and know there really, *really* was no chance. At least, that was what her brother told himself each time he kissed her goodbye.

This was a peculiar night, however. Very peculiar indeed. Tonight, at about a bit past midnight, the flower-like scar on the back of her neck started burning. Not that she could feel it, but the pale pink mark burned a bright red and glowed past her inky black hair.

There wasn't a window open in this hospital—the windows couldn't open—and no way to tell that a gentle breeze was drifting on by. Not until it passed through the open emergency doors and whooshed on by the paramedics rushing a car accident victim in.

You couldn't tell there was a breeze until it hit a wall, rolled over itself and around a corner, and strolled up to an emergency staircase and out on the fourth floor past the nurse's station, where a kind woman wrapped her sweater around herself tighter at the sudden chill. It took a right turn at the end of the hall and just slipped right in through the door cracked open.

And then you would be able to feel it, you would be able to feel that breeze. It was cold, yet astonishingly warm at the same time. It was a breeze that passes over you and makes you feel... astounded, like life was keeping secrets from you and they all just passed straight through you.

It was a breeze that brushed the inky hair off Jane's shoulder, curled up past her collar bone, snaked behind her neck, and made that flower rune burn a hot, searing white. You can't look right at it. You can't even be near it, but oh, god, was it beautiful.

There was no more breeze, no more answers to life's secrets. There was only silence and the steady beeping of the machine.

And then her eyes, burning a hot, vital green that nearly glowed into the dark space, fluttered open. Her machines hadn't roared to life yet. No monitors had picked up anything, but there was a white hot heat soaring through Jane's body now and a soul screaming from its depths.

Then the machines flared awake, a tumultuous sound of ringing bells and screaming technology alerting everyone within ten miles that the dead girl had woken up.

In those few moments, one of the last moments that she was left alone, Jane remembered a beautiful man with blue eyes kissing her, with calloused hands against the side of her face and sadness staining his features.

Then those green eyes melted back to their usual brown, and she was just a girl once more lying in a hospital bed with a tube down her throat.

She would dream of him, though... dream of a beautiful man in a beautiful town, and it would be the only thing she had for a long, long time.

Because Jane wasn't herself anymore, Jane was someone new.

And she needed to go home.

THE END

Can't get enough of Charlotte and Gabriel? Make sure you sign up for the author's blog to find out more about them!

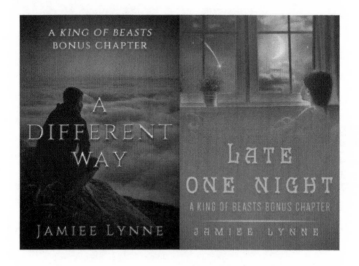

Get these two bonus chapters and more freebies when you sign up at jamiee.lynne.awesomeauthors.org!

Here is a sample from another story you may enjoy:

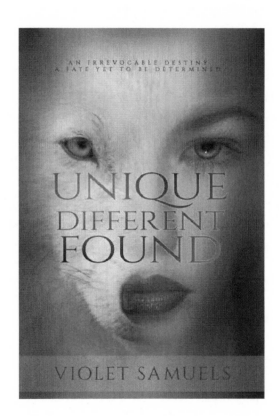

AN IRREVOCABLE DESTINY.
A FATE YET TO BE DETERMINED.

UNIQUE
DIFFERENT
FOUND

VIOLET SAMUELS

1

CELINA

Have you ever felt like you can never escape? Have you ever felt like there is no one there for you? Have you ever felt like the whole world is against you and you just want to get away and be free? Have you ever felt that you can never be loved or cherished?

That's my life.

I feel all of these things. You can't change what fate has in store for you. But sometimes, I wish I could just be free and live my own life. I haven't been able to do that for a total of nine years.

My mother and father died when I was seven. I was abandoned and left with my godforsaken pack. I had no regrets when my mother and father died. I spent every second of every day with them, and they never argued. We didn't have any major fights and we all loved each other so much. I didn't think my parents had any regrets either. I think they made the mistake of leaving me alone, though.

You're probably wondering why I'm blaming it on them, aren't you? Well, I don't. I blame my pack for being worthless, unfair, stupid and plain right mean. Childish I know, but true, down to the last detail. Every beating, every bruise, every broken bone and every possible evidence of them abusing me supports that horrid theory.

Ever since my parents died, I've been like a slave to the people I call my pack. I cook, wash, clean, organize and pretty much do everything for them. They throw away money like it's no big deal, and they don't spare a second glance to anyone who's 'lower' than them.

Someone like me.

All the wolves in my pack are gorgeous with either brown or blonde fur and have a mix of either blue, green, brown, or almost black eyes. Having plain blue or green eyes is rare. They have slim or muscular bodies and have the perfect height just to be much taller than humans. Unfortunately, that beauty is tainted by their bitter egos and cold hearts.

My parents were like the pack looks wise, but not personality wise. My parents were kind and thoughtful, always putting others before themselves. They never should've been in this pack in the first place.

The funny thing is, I look nothing like my parents or anyone in the pack for that matter.

Instead of blonde or brown hair, mine is pitch black, pin straight and comes down to just below my shoulders. My eyes are a shining gold that lost its shine many years ago, so now it looks like a light shade of mud. My lips are almost red and, strangely, my skin is pale. I'm not sure why... Most Werewolves have beautifully tanned skin. I'm also a bit shorter than everyone else, but I still have that slim body that anyone would die for. In my parents' opinion, being different is what makes you special. What makes you special, is what makes you unique.

I never believed it, though. All it has ever done was got me teased, and pushed around for being 'different' and 'unique'. It has always been like that. Even with my parents, they always said the pack was just jealous of my obvious beauty, one that I am oblivious to.

Another thing. When I turned sixteen, I made sure I was far away from the pack house, almost on the borders of our territory. The reason? I was shifting. I didn't want to give everyone the satisfaction of seeing my pain, and watching my every bone break after the other. I can honestly say that it is the most painful thing you will ever experience in your life.

When I shifted, I discovered that my wolf was snow white. Not one trace of colour other than white covered me. I was astounded. I had never seen a white wolf. Even my mother's and my father's wolves were brown and blonde, respectively. They told me that when I shifted, never to show to anyone my wolf unless they have my full trust. Nobody has.

I don't know what it means to have a pure white wolf, but I know that I'm different yet again. This time, in a way, I thought I could somehow fit into my pack. I thought wrong. When I came back, I got a beating because I was gone for most of the day, and everyone missed lunch and breakfast. That night, I had to make a three-course meal instead of the usual one, and I had to clean the house until it was spotless. Let's just say I stayed up way past midnight...

I haven't been for a run since. That was three weeks ago. My wolf has been howling in my head, and it feels like she's scratching my insides apart. I badly want to let her out, but I'm too scared. I don't want to get beaten up again.

My wolf has told me multiple times to get away, and I've been considering it for months now. Tonight's the night. I'm leaving. I'm ditching this stupid place and leaving for good. When I told my wolf, she was practically jumping with joy.

I'm making the dinner right now. Although this pack has treated me like nothing, I'm gonna give them something to remember me by, and if that means food, then so be it.

I decide to make one of my favourite courses. For entree, bruschetta with mini prawn cocktails. For main, lasagna with garlic bread. Then for dessert, my personal favourite, chocolate mud cake with whipped cream, ice cream and chocolate covered strawberries on top. If it were me, I would just skip the entree and main and go straight for the dessert.

I set the table for the pack, and as soon as I finish placing the last of the entrees on the table, they walk in through the door. As soon as they get a whiff, they come barging into the dining room, taking a seat and digging in. No 'thank you' or 'this is nice', just like the usual.

I always keep a spare bit of dessert for myself after I finish cooking, so while the rest of the pack eats, I tuck into my mud cake. At least, they let me eat, I guess.

When I hear the bell, I walk back out and collect the empty plates, taking them back to the kitchen. To let them digest a bit, I wash it all up and place it on the drying rack.

I come back out with the last of the mains and am about to walk out when Tina, the pack slut, calls my name.

"Celina!"

I slowly turn around, keeping my hands behind my back, and my head bowed. I'm wearing the correct uniform for serving dinner, and my hair is neatly pulled back into a high ponytail, so I'm not sure what she wants. Whenever someone in the pack calls my name, it's usually because I'm in trouble.

"Why the whole 'fancy-fancy' food? Is it a special occasion? Let me guess... Is it for Damon's birthday? A little present from you?" She snickers at me. I feel all eyes turn to me, but I obediently keep my head down. Damon is the soon to be the alpha of our pack and is turning eighteen in about four days. It's a big thing, and I'm supposed to cook for it...

"I guess you could consider it that. If the alpha is kind enough to accept my gift, of course," I answer in a small voice. I was told from the beginning to address Damon as alpha and nothing else, unlike the rest of the pack.

The room falls silent as every eye turns to Damon, who's sitting at the head of the very large dining table. I look through my long, black lashes to see his face. I'm met with a considering expression.

He nods his head once. "I accept your gift. I will expect a grander and more appropriate gift on my actual birthday, though. Do you understand?" His tone's filled with power and authority.

"Yes, Alpha, I understand," I say, returning to my former position with my head down.

"Good. Now, off you go." He shoos me off, and as soon as I enter the kitchen, I hear their laughs and snickers. I tried not to cry. I've shed too many tears over these heartless people.

They soon finish their meals, and it's time for dessert. I've finished mine by now, so I place theirs on the table with a blank face. They eat up and by the time everyone has finished and has stayed around talking, I've cleared the large table and washed up.

I enter back into the dining room and wait in my usual spot by the door of the kitchen. Every night before I go to bed, I either get hit or nothing for the meals I've cooked. It's the same with breakfast, lunch, and any other meals they eat. As each one walks out of the room, I either get shoved or ignored, which means they liked my cooking. Tina, on the other hand, slaps me across the face. You probably think that's harsh, but that's equivalent to someone else's shove. So just imagine what someone else's slap is to her. It's not a pretty sight.

Damon is the last to leave, and he stops in front of me. I cautiously lift my head and stare into his beautiful blue-green eyes. He has a blank face, as do I. We stare at each other for a moment before he walks out and leaves me alone in the dining room to fix up.

Damon has been my crush since I was about ten, even though he treats me like the worthless thing I am. His brown hair and blue-green eyes are the main aspects that draw me and many other female wolves in. He hasn't found his mate yet either, which means he's available. He wouldn't go for me, though. Not in a million years. I'm too different.

I head to bed in the early hours of the night. The pack no longer requires me after about 7:30 pm, so I am ordered to bed, which I quickly oblige, so as not to get beaten. I still have bruises from the worst ones.

The sad thing is, I believe everything my pack had said since my parents died. That I'm not beautiful, but ugly. That I'm not unique, but different. That I'm not a part of their family, but their slave.

I sigh as I enter my makeshift room. It's bare, except for a large window that lets the moonlight from the full moon flood into my room. My bed is pretty much a sheet on the hard, splintered, wooden floor, and my pillow is a pillow cover stuffed with newspaper.

I won't be sleeping there tonight, though. Not anymore. Not ever again.

I pack what little belongings I have inside a sack – A pair of worn out jeans, an oversized shirt with holes in it, a skirt, one other shirt that appears to be clean, and a pair of socks. I don't own any shoes.

I grab the only piece of jewellery I have, my mother's silver necklace with her and my father's names engraved into the heart-shaped pendant. The pendant has a yin and yang symbol in it, but it's made with little black and white crystals. I slip it into my shirt and proceed to the window.

I open it wide, and without a glance back, or second thought, I jump. I jump to my freedom and my new life.

I shift into my snow white wolf and take off with my sack in my mouth. I don't know where I'm going. I don't know if I can survive. I am only a newly shifted wolf at the age of sixteen.

What do I know? I'll never have to see my 'pack' again. That is enough to make me smile slightly in my wolf form. As I cross the border of the territory, my wolf lets out a howl, filled with happiness and joy.

We're free. I'm free.

Never again will we have to face the Moonlight pack.

If you enjoyed this sample then look for **Unique Different Found** on Amazon!

Other books you might enjoy:

Break Me, Mate
Nique Joaquin
Available on Amazon!

Other books you might enjoy:

Purr, Kitten
Kristel Juurik
Available on Amazon!

Introducing the Characters Magazine App

Download the app to get the free issues of interviews from famous fiction characters and find your next favorite book!

iTunes: bit.ly/CharactersApple
Google Play: bit.ly/CharactersAndroid

Acknowledgements

Thank you to all my fans for your continued support throughout my book's writing process and its publication. The completion of this book would not have been possible without you by my side.

Thank you to my publisher and all the people who played a vital role in editing and stylizing my book along with getting it to where it is now. You've made my dream of becoming a published author come true, and I can't be more grateful.

A huge thanks to my sister, Haley, for sticking by my side while writing and being the only one I really trusted to see my work before anyone else. You were the encouragement I needed through my countless breaks in self-esteem. Thank you eternally.

And thanks to my dog for keeping my feet warm while I wrote and giving me his silent thoughts when I read him each draft.

Author's Note

Hey there!

Thank you so much for reading King of Beasts! I can't express how grateful I am for reading something that was once just a thought inside my head.

I'd love to hear from you! Please feel free to email me at jamiee_lynne@awesomeauthors.org and sign up at jamiee.lynne.awesomeauthors.org for freebies!

One last thing: I'd love to hear your thoughts on the book. Please leave a review on Amazon or Goodreads because I just love reading your comments and getting to know YOU!

Whether that review is good or bad, I'd still love to hear it!

Can't wait to hear from you!

JAMIEE LYNNE

About the Author

Jamie Roy is an American born author in pursuit of her goals to become not only a writer, but a chemist. Aided by her golden retriever and a never ending ambition, she hopes to continue going through life with the eye of a scientist and the mind of an author.

89316638R00142

Made in the USA
Middletown, DE
15 September 2018